"Are you feeling relaxed yet?"

"Far from it." Travis almost groaned the answer to Jenna's question.

Her lips were swollen and her eyes half-lidded as she smiled up at him. "Guess I'll have to try a little harder, then."

"If you try any harder, the last thing I'll be is relaxed."

She bit her lower lip, then slowly released it and sighed. "We'd better be going, hmm?"

Going where? Oh, right, to the country house. Travis tore his gaze away from Jenna.

"Yeah, we'd better. I think we're still a half hour away." But if they happened to pass a hotel along the way, he wasn't sure he'd be able to keep himself from screeching into the lot and dragging Jenna to the nearest available room.

An image of making love to her on a cheap bedspread in a sleazy motel room flashed in his mind, and he banished it. How had he gone so quickly from respectable businessman to crazed guy who got in bar fights and fantasized about frenzied motel sex?

He looked back at Jenna, and he knew in an instant.

Dear Reader,

I've always admired women who aren't afraid to take risks to get what they want. With this book, I've had the pleasure of writing about just such a woman. Jenna Calvert is a journalist who isn't afraid of much—except the stalker trying to stop her from writing the story of her career. I only wish I were half as bold as Jenna.

I can relate more easily to the hero, Travis Roth, who finds his perfectly planned life shaken up by wild, unpredictable Jenna. When these two come together, they illustrate why opposites can make the very best lovers.

I hope you love reading Travis and Jenna's wild journey as much as I loved writing it. You can drop me a note to let me know what you think of the story at jamie@jamiesobrato.com or visit my Web site, www.jamiesobrato.com, to find out more about my upcoming books.

Sincerely,

Jamie Sobrato

Books by Jamie Sobrato

HARLEQUIN TEMPTATION
911—SOME LIKE IT SIZZLING

HARLEQUIN BLAZE
 84—PLEASURE FOR PLEASURE
116—WHAT A GIRL WANTS
133—SOME KIND OF SEXY

JAMIE
SOBRATO

TOO WILD

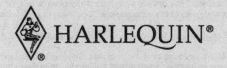

TORONTO • NEW YORK • LONDON
AMSTERDAM • PARIS • SYDNEY • HAMBURG
STOCKHOLM • ATHENS • TOKYO • MILAN • MADRID
PRAGUE • WARSAW • BUDAPEST • AUCKLAND

To The Wild Writers, who've been there for me
from the start. I'm blessed to have the friendship and support
of such a wild, wonderful group of women.

ISBN 0-373-69197-1

TOO WILD

Copyright © 2004 by Jamie Sobrato.

This edition published by arrangement with Harlequin Books S.A.

www.eHarlequin.com

Printed in U.S.A.

1

WHAT JENNA CALVERT NEEDED was a large, tattooed man with a look of death in his eyes. Perhaps someone with a prison record and an intimate knowledge of firearms. Some guy named Spike or Duff.

But even Bodyguards for Less was out of her price range. Jenna listened a second time to the phone recording that described the business's services. No way could she swing the eighty dollars per hour the burly voice on the recording stated was the base price without additional services—and what additional services could a bodyguard provide, anyway?

She hung up and exhaled a ragged breath.

Without a bodyguard, the only protection she had was Guard-Dog-In-A-Box. For twenty-nine dollars and ninety-nine cents, she'd purchased as much peace of mind as she could afford—a sorry amount indeed. Thirty bucks had bought her a motion-sensing device that simulated the sounds of killer dogs barking at any unsuspecting intruders.

Unfortunately, it also barked at neighbors passing in the hallway, at pizza delivery men and at Mrs.

Lupinski's many elderly lovers traipsing in and out of the building at all hours of the day and night.

Jenna hadn't had a good night's sleep in a week, and everyone else in the building was getting tired of her canned guard dogs, too. Even Mrs. Lupinski, who was normally otherwise engaged, had yelled obscenities out her door at Jenna last night when she had heard her in the stairwell.

Guard-Dog-In-A-Box had looked so promising there on the shelf at the store, but now that she'd lived with her faux protection for a week, she saw just how desperate she'd become to even buy it.

She was cooked meat.

She never should have started researching the underbelly of the beauty-pageant industry. Ever since she'd begun the research a month ago, her life had been turned upside down by someone who didn't want her writing the story. Jenna had racked her brain trying to figure out who among the people she'd interviewed or spoken with might wish her harm, but no one jumped out as a likely culprit. She hadn't even uncovered any information that seemed worthy of death threats. But the voice-altered phone calls and the threatening mail had included comments like "back off the story" and "you're risking your life if you write it."

Jenna surveyed her apartment, wishing now that she had a roommate, or at least a parakeet. Someone to comfort her and tell her that it wasn't such a bad thing to get three death threats in the past month. Someone who could also remind her that it was really quite normal to nearly get run down by a car in San Francisco. Two days in a row.

Yes, a roommate would be nice right about now. A roommate, a bodyguard and a really big weapon. But all Jenna had was Guard-Dog-In-A-Box. She resisted the urge to hurl the waste of money across the room and eyed the double locks on the apartment door. If anyone really wanted to get in, they wouldn't have much trouble. The wood of the door frame was rotting away in places, and the locks looked as if they'd been installed before Jenna was born.

Sure, the front door of her apartment building was supposed to remain locked to nonresidents, but Mrs. Lupinski liked to prop it open for her lovers and the ever anticipated sweepstakes-prize delivery people. Getting buzzed in on the rare occasions it was locked was as easy as claiming to be a pizza delivery guy.

Jenna leaned against the decrepit door and closed her eyes. She let her mind drift to happier days, when home security was the least of her concerns. Only two months ago she'd been a relatively carefree journalist who'd made a decent career of writing for women's magazines, and she was embarking on the story she was sure would finally turn her career from decent to well paying. No more squeaking by on a paltry freelance income that barely paid the high rent in the city. The beauty-pageant exposé was supposed to be her ticket to success.

When the buzzer on the door sounded, she jumped so hard that Guard-Dog-In-A-Box clattered to the floor and began barking. It sounded about as menacing as tin-can recorded dog barks could sound—that is, not menacing at all.

Her hand shook as she pressed the intercom button and said, "Who is it?"

"Ms. Calvert? My name is Travis Roth. I need to talk to you about your sister, Kathryn. May I come up?"

Kathryn? Jenna stared at the intercom, dumbfounded. She hadn't heard from or spoken to her twin sister in years. Could this be a ploy someone was using to get inside the building?

"What about her? Just tell me now."

"I really need to speak with you face-to-face. It's a sensitive matter."

A sensitive matter? Did bloodthirsty criminals talk like that?

"Haven't you ever heard of the telephone?"

"I've been trying to call you for days with no answer."

Oh. Right. She'd unplugged the answering machine after the strange calls started coming in, and finally she'd just stopped answering the phone.

"Look, if you're here about the pageant story, I don't have any idea what your problem is with it!"

She turned off the intercom and pushed her sofa against the door, then climbed on top of it and pulled her legs to her chest. She was beginning to think journalism had been the wrong career choice. What she needed was a nice, safe job. Maybe in forestry, or library science.

No, that was just fear talking. She loved her work. She'd always dreamed of being a freelance writer, and now she was one. Was she really such a coward she'd let someone bully her out of writing the truth? Scared as she might be, in her gut, Jenna knew she wasn't about to stop working on the article.

Fifteen minutes later, she was still sitting in the same spot staring at her chipped toenail polish when she heard Mrs. Lupinski hollering about the whereabouts of her free pizza, a sure sign that the guy with the sensitive matter to discuss had gotten into the building.

Someone knocked at the door, and in spite of herself Jenna jumped again.

"Ms. Calvert, this is urgent. It's about your sister's wedding."

Kathryn was getting married? No surprise there, if he was telling the truth. Her sister had been dreaming of a rich Prince Charming ever since they'd been old enough to date.

"She needs your help."

"Right, now I know you're lying. And why isn't she here asking for my help herself if she needs it?" Kathryn would no sooner ask for Jenna's help than she would wear a designer knockoff dress.

"I'll explain, if you'll just give me a chance."

"Go away before I call the police!"

She peered through the peephole at him to see his reaction. Yow! What a cutie. Smoky green eyes, sand-colored hair streaked with blond and cut meticulously short, the kind of stern, masculine mouth that begged to be kissed into submission. Not exactly the face of a thug, but what did she know? Maybe criminals were going for the *GQ* look this year.

"I understand you and Kathryn haven't spoken in some time, and you didn't part on friendly terms."

Okay, somehow he'd found some personal information to make his cover seem authentic. Jenna sank back down on the couch and chewed her lip.

"Jenna, this is really urgent. Open the door."

She eyed the fire escape. Today was not a good day to die. For one thing, her roots were starting to show, and she had a zit on her chin. She'd look like hell in a casket. Maybe this guy was legit, but she couldn't afford to find out. It would only be a short drop from the bottom of the fire escape to the ground.

She hopped off the couch, grabbed her backpack purse, slid her feet into the nearest pair of sandals and hurried to the fire-escape window.

The gorgeous maybe-assassin started pounding on the door, and Jenna pushed her window open and squeezed through it. Her breath came out ragged, and she imagined herself in an action movie as she climbed down the fire escape and dangled herself over the bottom edge for the drop. Five feet, no problem. She let go and landed with a thud in the scraggly mess of weeds that made up her building's backyard vegetation.

Now what? She hadn't exactly formulated an escape plan. Jenna eyed the tall chain-link fence that surrounded the backyard and tried to envision herself scaling it. No way—she wasn't risking it unless there were no other options.

If she hurried, she might be able to go out the alleyway to the street and slip away before he realized she wasn't in her apartment anymore. Jenna hurried to the rusty gate and eased it open, then ran down the alley to the sidewalk.

She'd only made it past the neighbor's house when she heard a man's voice call after her, "Jenna, wait!"

Him again. What, did he have X-ray vision? Jenna ran, and the sound of footsteps quickened. He caught up with her as she rounded the corner of the next street.

"Kathryn said you'd resist helping, but she didn't tell me you were crazy," he said over her shoulder, and something about the perplexed tone of his voice made Jenna stop and look at him.

He was even more gorgeous in person without his features distorted by the peephole. Up close, he was half a foot taller than her, and he stood with the kind of assurance that suggested he was accustomed to being in charge. Jenna's fear was suddenly overcome with a pang of desire. Wow, did she ever need to pay more attention to her love life, if her would-be assassin was suddenly turning her on.

His clothes—a navy wool sport coat, an open-collared white oxford and a pair of beige summer wool slacks—were tailored, expensive. The way they fit, the way he looked so carefully put to-gether, gave Jenna the urge to muss him up.

He was studying her, probably trying to make sense of the differences between herself and her high-society identical twin. "You *are* Jenna Calvert, right?"

Jenna kept her hair long and dyed various shades of red—this month it was Auburn Fire—while Kathryn had always been fond of short deb-utante haircuts in their natural blond color. And Jenna had always asserted her independence and uniqueness from her twin through her wild ward-robe, while Kathryn's taste tended toward the classic and exorbitantly priced.

"Yes," she said, secretly thrilled that she'd man-aged to distinguish herself from her identical twin so well.

"I'm Travis Roth. It's good to finally meet you." He withdrew a business card from his pocket and offered it to her. Jenna took it and read the raised black lettering on a tasteful white linen card. Travis Roth, CEO, Roth Investments.

Whoopee. Any bozo could get business cards made up and call himself a CEO.

Jenna stuck it in her pocket.

"What color are Kathryn's bridesmaid dresses going to be?"

"Excuse me?"

"The colors in the wedding—dresses, flowers, everything. If you know that, I'll talk to you."

He appeared to be giving the matter some thought. "I'm afraid I don't know."

Jenna wished she'd remembered to grab a kitchen knife on the way out the window. "If you know Kathryn, you'd know what colors are in her wedding."

A look of understanding softened his features. "Some kind of purple? Lavender, right?"

Lavender was Kathryn's signature color. Ever since they were kids, she'd worn lavender, while Jenna'd had to wear identical outfits in pink. But that was one of their many differences—Kathryn had embraced being dressed up as a sideshow act by their mother, while Jenna had hated every moment of it. She still couldn't look at the color pink without feeling slightly nauseated.

Kathryn could never understand why Jenna had felt the need to differentiate herself from her twin with wild clothes and different hair colors, while Jenna couldn't understand her twin's obsession with being one of an identical pair.

"Okay, so what's your connection to my sister and her wedding?"

"I'm her fiancé's brother, and I'll explain everything if you'll just give me a half hour of your time."

Her curiosity was piqued now that she had some assurance this Travis guy wasn't a hardened criminal. What sort of urgent matter could bring Kathryn to turn to Jenna for help? And why had she sent her fiancé's brother to talk to her?

She looked Travis up and down. Okay, considering his sex appeal, he was a pretty good messenger. She could stand to spend a half hour with him, though she could think of much more interesting things to do with him than talk about Kathryn and her prenuptial problems.

"I'll listen, if you'll buy lunch," she said, her stomach rumbling because she'd skipped breakfast. "There's a diner around the corner."

TRAVIS DID HIS VERY BEST to focus on the business at hand, but Jenna Calvert had thrown him completely off track. She wasn't at all what he'd expected. Yes, Kathryn had described her as a rebellious type, as someone who liked to shock others and be contrary just for the sake of conflict, but she hadn't mentioned how damn sexy Jenna would be.

A waitress with three nose rings and threads of purple in her braided hair arrived to take their order, and Travis tried to take his mind off Jenna long enough to choose a lunch. His gaze landed on meat loaf, and he wasn't sure if he'd ever even tasted it, but he'd seen it on TV and decided that's what he was having.

"I'll have the meat loaf, and…" Certainly wine wasn't the appropriate beverage. "Iced tea."

"You want green tea or black?" This was San Francisco, after all.

"Green will be fine."

He caught himself staring at Jenna's lush pink lips as she placed her own order for a cheeseburger, chili fries and a chocolate shake, and when the waitress disappeared, he forced his gaze back to Jenna's eyes.

The gorgeous redhead had managed in the space of ten minutes to muddle his thoughts and set his senses on high alert. It took a monumental effort to keep from letting his gaze fall even lower than her sensuous mouth to the front of her tight black tank top—to keep from thinking about the fact that she apparently wasn't wearing a bra.

And curse the guy who invented bras if all women could look like that without them.

She wasn't even remotely his type. Her look wasn't classic Coco Chanel, as he'd always preferred, but rather rebel-without-a-Nordstrom-card. With her dyed burgundy hair; her short, unpolished fingernails and her tight, faded jeans, she was about as opposite to Kathryn Calvert as she could get and still be the woman's twin sister.

When he looked into her ice-blue eyes, he saw sparks of fire that weren't present in her sister's. Perhaps Jenna had spirit, something he suspected lacking in Kathryn. Travis was undeniably intrigued by this wilder twin, and he was curious to know her in spite of his suspicion that she probably had a tattoo hiding somewhere on her body.

Where and what that tattoo might be—the possibilities were endless. A little red rose on the satin skin of her inner thigh, or a tiny heart hiding beneath her panties… Whoa, mama.

What on earth was going on here? He didn't like tattoos, and he didn't even know if Jenna had one. But she certainly had his imagination in the gutter all of a sudden.

There was no sense in fantasizing about Kathryn's bad-girl twin anyway, because if she agreed to his offer—and he knew she would—then she would be transformed in the next few days into an exact replica of her sister. It was his unwelcome job to make that happen.

Jenna sat across from him with her elbows propped on the table, her slender arms sporting two chunky bracelets in various stones and faux gems, displaying an utter lack of grace that Travis found oddly charming. As he explained his acquaintance with Kathryn Calvert and her engagement to his younger brother, Blake, she listened closely, never taking her gaze away from his eyes.

But next came the sensitive part, the reason he'd driven all the way from Carmel in the hope of bringing Jenna back with him.

"The wedding plans were moving along just fine until last week, when Kathryn flew to Los Angeles for what she claims was supposed to be a week-long spa treatment. She decided to get some minor plastic surgery while she was there, and—"

"What kind of plastic surgery?" Jenna's eyes had grown perfectly round.

Their conversation was interrupted by the waitress delivering their meals and drinks. Jenna continued to watch him as she dug into her burger.

When the waitress left, Travis continued. "Some kind of procedure where the doctor takes fat from one part of your body and injects it into the cheeks and lips. Kathryn is outraged with the results, and she refuses to come home until the problem has been corrected."

Jenna laughed out loud. "What, her face is too fat now?"

Travis smiled. "Something like that. She says she looks lumpy." He couldn't begin to understand why anyone would endure such a procedure, especially not for beauty's sake, but of all the people he knew, Kathryn was the easiest to imagine having fat injected into her face.

"Now I've heard it all."

"The problem is, we can't postpone the wedding or any of the prenuptial events. For one thing, Kathryn doesn't want my family to know she was off having facial enhancements done. My mother hasn't exactly welcomed her into the family."

"I can imagine how important it is for Kathryn to impress her future mother-in-law."

"She has a long list of people to impress, I'm afraid. Kathryn initiated a project with Blake to establish a women and children's shelter through the Roth charity foundation, and she is supposed to meet with a couple interested in donating land for the project later this week."

"So reschedule."

"They're already hesitant about the project thanks to Blake's reputation for flakiness. Kathryn doesn't want to give them any reason to back out, because such a prime piece of land so central to the Bay Area is nearly impossible to come by."

Jenna frowned. "Sounds like she's got herself in a real bind."

"Not just herself, but my business, too. Our family's investment firm has suffered recently as a result of Blake's inability to handle responsibility, and this wedding is our chance to give some of our clients a better impression of him, to leave them feeling warm and fuzzy about Roth Investments. We need everything to come off without a hitch."

Jenna's expression turned wary as she bit into a French fry. "Why can't you just tell everyone that the bride has come down with pneumonia or something and is too sick to go through with the wedding?"

Travis took his first bite of meat loaf and decided he'd been missing out all these years. He made a mental note to ask the family chef to prepare the dish regularly.

"Any postponement will look like flakiness on the family's part, no matter what the excuse, and that's an image we have to avoid at all costs. Several of our biggest clients have threatened to leave because of Blake's unreliability. This marriage will show them that he's settling down and becoming a family man."

"Why doesn't someone just fire your brother?"

If it were only so easy. "My father has forbidden it. Blake is Dad's favorite."

"This all sounds a little crazy, and I don't understand how you think I can help."

"The doctors have assured Kathryn that her face will look normal before the wedding, but she still refuses to come home until the damage has been undone."

"So you just have to hope she'll come back in time for it."

"And that's exactly what I'm doing, except that still leaves us without a bride for the prewedding events my parents have planned, along with the land donation meeting."

"Does your brother know about Kathryn's little problem?"

"No, and he cannot find out. He's awful at keeping anything secret. He's expecting Kathryn back from her trip on Monday, but she obviously won't be back."

"Isn't he going to notice when his bride doesn't show up for the rehearsal?"

Travis took a deep breath. "That's where you come in. We need you to impersonate Kathryn until she returns."

Jenna dropped her cheeseburger onto its plate and stared at him as if he'd just sprouted antennae.

"You're out of your mind," she said matter-of-factly, her cheek full of half-chewed cheeseburger.

"You haven't even heard my offer yet."

"Sorry to disappoint you, but I'm not going to help Kathryn or the dimwit who agreed to marry her."

Kathryn had never explained why she and Jenna were estranged from each other. Apparently the rift was a deep one, judging by Jenna's reaction, but Kathryn had mentioned how she and her twin had switched places many times as children—how it had in fact been one of their favorite games.

"You'll be quite well compensated." He noted a gleam of interest in her eye that she quickly subdued.

"I'm earning a good living already. I don't need anyone's charity."

From the looks of Jenna's neighborhood, Travis was willing to bet she was barely scraping by on her meager freelance earnings, and that she could definitely use the money he had to offer.

"Not charity. Payment for a job completed."

"Yeah, whatever. I still won't do it."

"You don't even know what the compensation will be."

"Not enough." She turned her attention to her milk shake.

He could tell by the tenseness in her narrow

shoulders that he had to pull his final punch. "Twenty-five thousand dollars."

Chocolate milk shake spurted from her mouth across the table and onto the lapel of his favorite jacket. She stared at him wild-eyed.

He dipped his napkin into a glass of ice water and dabbed at the spot until it disappeared, and when he looked back up, she was scooting out of the booth.

"Where are you going?"

"Away from you and whatever crooked scheme you've cooked up." She stood and shrugged on her small leather backpack.

Travis stared after her as she headed for the door.

He hadn't anticipated her walking away once he'd started to talk money. Nor had he imagined he'd be so mesmerized by the sway of her hips in those faded Levi's that he'd be frozen in place, speechless and unable to form complete thoughts. No, things weren't going the way he'd planned at all.

2

JENNA CLIMBED THE STAIRS to her apartment, her
mind playing over and over Travis's proposal.
Had she made too rash a decision? Twenty-five
grand was a lot of money to walk away from, yet
the thought of not only helping Kathryn, but actually taking over her life, was just too much to
contemplate all at once.

Jenna had spent every moment since she'd left
home ten years ago trying to forget that she was
not unique in the world, that she had an identical
twin out there and that she wasn't even the best
liked of the two. Kathryn had always been their
parents' favorite, their teachers' favorite and the
one who had more friends and more boyfriends.
Kathryn knew the art of getting along to get along,
while Jenna had been born with a rebellious streak
that angered authority figures and scared away
the faint of heart.

An image of Travis Roth popped into her head.
A perverse little part of her wondered if he was
faint of heart, or if he'd be the kind of guy who
could hang on when life with Jenna got unpredict-

able. Crazy thoughts, considering a guy like Travis and a girl like Jenna would never get together, not in a thousand years—unless, of course, some sort of paid services were involved.

Like being hired to impersonate her sister.

The thought gave Jenna a shudder. Impersonating Kathryn would be like taking a giant leap backward in time. She'd be admitting that all her rebellion in the past ten years had been for nothing—that with a bottle of dye, some scissors, a change of clothes and a bit of makeup, she was just a duplicate of her ever-so-proper sister.

The wild hairstyles, the sexy clothes, the wild men, the wild nights out...

All for nothing.

The choices she'd made to prove herself an individual could be wiped away in one fell swoop.

Jenna reached her floor of the apartment building, and the first thing she saw was her door standing ajar. She froze, and her stomach contracted into a rock.

Could Travis have gotten it open before he came outside and found her trying to escape? Possible, but how could he have so quickly gotten around the couch she'd jammed up against it earlier? That, along with getting past the locks, would have taken more time than he'd had to come back outside and catch her sneaking away.

She took a step closer and saw that the locks hadn't been broken, and an image of the open fire-escape window flashed in her mind. In this neighborhood, no one left fire-escape windows open unless they wanted to find all their valuables and not-so-valuables for sale at a swap meet the next weekend.

Her heart raced. Should she go in or just leave and call the police from a neighbor's place? Common sense told her to leave, but curiosity had her aching to peek inside, if only for a moment.

Her computer—she had to know that it was safe.

Jenna held her breath and stepped into the doorway, thinking of how she was going to pitch Guard-Dog-In-A-Box out the window at Travis Roth's head if she saw him outside her building again. Slowly, she eased her head around the half-open door, until she could see the interior of the apartment.

It took her a moment to make sense of the changes since she'd last been there an hour ago. Couch overturned, cushions ripped open, papers and books strewn everywhere, bookshelves emptied and her laptop missing from her desk.

Jenna's heart pounded in her ears as she realized the months—the *years*—of work saved on her hard drive that now might be missing, and she didn't see her box of floppy disks anywhere among the mess.

She gripped the door frame and resisted the urge to rush in and search for her laptop and files before she knew for sure that the intruder was gone. She needed to think, make a plan…. First she'd go to Mrs. Lupinski's and ask to use the phone.

She backed away from the door and crept up the stairs.

Damn it.

Was Travis Roth a diversion for someone to break into her apartment? No, that didn't make sense. He hadn't come expecting that she'd flee out the window, that they'd end up having lunch at a diner down the street... But he could have had some other plan to get her out of the apartment. Could that whole story about her sister have been an elaborate charade?

Her mind raced from thought to thought, and her hands began to shake as the reality of what she'd likely just lost sank in.

Jenna raised her fist to knock on Mrs. Lupinski's door, but the door swung open at that moment and her neighbor, in mint-green curlers and a red satin robe, peered out.

"Shouldn't have left your window open, huh! Saw some guy climbing up the fire escape, and twenty minutes later he walked right out the front carrying a black bag full of stuff."

"Did you call the police?"

"How was I supposed to know if he was up to no-good? Could have been a friend of yours for all I knew." Mrs. Lupinski's robe slid open in the front to reveal a black lace nightgown. The sounds of a daytime soap opera could be heard in the background.

Jenna shuddered. She knew better than to argue with her cantankerous neighbor. "I need to use your phone. My apartment has been robbed and ransacked." *While you were up here minding your own business.*

Damn it, damn it, damn it.

She wanted to throw up or kick something. Or both. Tears burned her eyes, but she blinked them away, determined not to let her neighbor see how upset she really was.

The elderly woman eyed her suspiciously but stepped aside and motioned her in. Jenna had never actually been inside the apartment before, and she half expected to see a heart-shaped bed in the living room, mirrors on the ceiling, maybe a few pieces of emergency resuscitation equipment in case any of her lovers went into cardiac arrest at an inopportune moment.

What she saw instead was a two-room flat almost identical to her own, except for the matter of décor. Mrs. Lupinski had stopped decorating sometime in the late sixties, when she'd apparently been enamored with orange-and-green flower prints.

She pointed to a telephone next to the couch, and Jenna was surprised to note that it actually had a rotary dial. The feel of catching her shaky fingers in the small holes as she dialed 911 took her back to childhood for a fleeting moment, until an operator came on the line and she found herself recounting the relevant details of the break-in.

The operator warned her not to enter her apartment again until the police had secured it, so Jenna was stuck waiting for them to arrive in the company of Mrs. Lupinski. Luckily, her neighbor didn't see any need for small talk. Without saying a word, she simply planted herself in front of the TV and watched with undivided attention the plight of Rafe and Savannah, a couple who seemed to be very upset over the resurrection of someone named Lucius.

Jenna, left to her own thoughts, didn't want to consider what might be missing from her meager belongings. Nor did she want to contemplate whether the break-in was connected to her research of the pageant industry. If it was, and if her files were missing—

A sense of violation rose up in her chest. *How could they?* How could someone have taken her things, violated her privacy, stolen her work—the thing that mattered most to her?

It was bad enough that she'd taken to cowering behind her apartment door, afraid to venture out in public like a normal person. Now her home had been invaded, and she had nowhere to cower.

No, she had to stop thinking this way. This was exactly the kind of fear they wanted her to succumb to.

She shook herself mentally and her thoughts landed instead on Travis Roth. Where did he fit into this puzzle? Her gut told her he was telling the truth, and her libido told her he was an undeniable babe. But what if he were a hit man, hired

to lure her away and kill her, then dump her body
in a shallow grave? There was one way to find
out, even if it meant calling her mother, Irene
Calvert-Hathaway.

She picked up the phone again, dialed direct-
ory assistance, and went through the motions of
placing a collect call to Palm Springs. Moments
later, she heard her mother's voice on the line. It
should have been a comforting sound, in light of
the circumstances.

"Mom, it's Jenna."

"What's the matter, dear? Are you dead? Did
you get thrown in jail?"

"No, Mom. If I were dead, I'd have trouble di-
aling the phone. My apartment was just broken
into and I can't go back in yet, but that's not why
I'm calling."

She heard her mother's put-upon sigh. "I told
you not to move to that crazy city. Probably drug
addicts—I've read how they steal things to support their habits."

"I'm calling about Kathryn, actually. I hear
she's getting married."

"To an absolutely magnificent man!" Her mother's voice had changed from nagging to dreamy
in an instant. "The wedding is in two weeks. I told
Kathryn to send you an invitation, but the way
you two fight…"

Yeah, yeah, whatever. No need to invite the
black sheep of the family to the social event of the
season. Kathryn probably couldn't imagine her

lowlife sister rubbing elbows with her country-club friends. Not that Jenna considered herself a lowlife, but she knew her lack of a six-figure income and her less than glamorous lifestyle were a major embarrassment to her family.

While Kathryn had stepped right into their mother's social climbing footsteps, Jenna had never been much impressed by status symbols and excessive wealth. Her rejection of the material life was a constant source of discord between herself and her family, and Jenna imagined Kathryn and their mother shaking their heads and tut-tutting every time the subject of Jenna's rattletrap car or seedy apartment came up.

"It doesn't matter. Do you know anything about Travis Roth, the brother of Kathryn's fiancé?"

She could almost see her mother's surgically youthful eyes narrow. "Why do you ask, dear?"

"He, or someone claiming to be him, contacted me today."

"About what?"

"First, tell me what you know about him," Jenna said, already feeling relieved that at least there *was* a Travis Roth.

"I've only met him a few times, but he seemed like quite the gentleman. Handsome, too. He has a stellar reputation, from what I hear. Runs the investment branch of the Roth family empire, isn't married, lives in Carmel near his brother and their parents."

"What does he look like, exactly?"

"Tall, sandy blond hair, green eyes, nice physique, in his mid-thirties."

"Do you happen to know if their family is connected to any beauty pageants?"

"No, and why on earth do you ask?"

"Never mind." Jenna relaxed back onto the sofa, releasing a mental sigh of relief. It sounded as if her lunch companion wasn't a fraud and knew nothing about the break-in.

"What are all these questions about?"

"I can't say, but don't worry. I'm not going to ruin Kathryn's wedding or anything."

Soon after Jenna ended the call with her mother, the police arrived, checked out her apartment, took statements from Jenna and Mrs. Lupinski and dusted for fingerprints. The biggest clue the police found was a note scrawled on the bathroom mirror in red lipstick that read, "Don't write the story, bitch."

The only story Jenna was working on was the beauty-pageant exposé, so she'd given the police all the information she could remember about whom she had contacted during her research and promised to let them know if she remembered anything else. They'd advised her to take some time off and leave town, maybe stay with family or friends, but to give them an address and phone number for wherever she went.

An hour after they'd left, Jenna sat alone in her ransacked apartment, nervous and depressed. Her laptop and all her files had indeed been stolen.

She didn't allow herself to think about the years of work that were now gone. Instead, she focused on the mess. She wandered around and around the small space surveying her once orderly surroundings.

And strangely, her thoughts kept going back to Travis Roth. His offer wasn't sounding so outrageous, now that her normal life had suddenly turned into a bad dream she wanted to wake from. As if she hadn't been scared enough before, now she knew for absolute sure that someone didn't want her writing the beauty-pageant exposé.

Jenna twirled a strand of hair between her fingers in a nervous habit she'd engaged in since childhood. Any minute now, she figured her eye would start twitching, and then some outrageous behavior wouldn't be far behind.

Her entire life, she'd always relieved tension by doing something wild. In elementary school, there'd been that incident with Mrs. Joliet's desk chair right before the big Little Miss Twin America finals. In junior high, there had been the liberation of the science-class rats after her mother had filed for divorce from her father. In high school, there'd been the time she'd cut class and gone cruising with the biggest badass hunk in school, right before refusing to ever do another beauty pageant.

Later, she'd discovered a little fun in bed had the same effect. Preferably, outrageous fun in bed. And here she was with the greatest need for a tension reliever she'd ever had, and no boyfriend or even the prospect of one in sight.

Jenna sank onto her bed, fighting back the big melodramatic sob that threatened to escape her throat.

Not now, not when she had to think.

Two weeks and twenty-five thousand dollars. She'd get to leave town, forget about her own mess of a life for a little while. Maybe that would give the police enough time to catch the scumbag who'd just trashed her apartment. Or maybe not.

But she'd get to leave town. Even if it meant impersonating her sister, perpetrating a fraud, it was an offer she couldn't turn down now.

And maybe the offer had advantages she hadn't even considered yet. She envisioned Travis Roth in all his tall, blond, broad-shouldered, suntanned glory. Maybe a few weeks in close proximity to him was just what she needed…and maybe a little negotiating was called for.

She smiled, and an outrageous impulse came bubbling up from her subconscious.

Negotiations, yes.

Something to take her mind off her worries. Something to remind her that she was still Jenna, still in control of her own destiny.

Something wild.

Yes.

A calm settled over her for the first time since she'd laid eyes on her ransacked apartment, and an idea formed in her head. An outrageous idea, guaranteed to make her forget her problems, sure to dwarf all the other outrageous stunts she'd pulled over the years.

She withdrew Travis's business card from her pocket and stared at it. After a few moments and a silent prayer, Jenna dialed his number.

TRAVIS HAD DECIDED to drop in on an old college friend at his office downtown before leaving the city. He was just starting the car, wondering what his next step with regard to Jenna should be, when his cell phone rang.

"Travis Roth," he answered.

"It's Jenna Calvert. I've been thinking about your offer, and I may have changed my mind."

"So you're willing to help?"

"Maybe. I have a condition of my own I'd like to discuss, in person."

"Of course. I'm open to negotiating."

"I'd like you to come here to my apartment and pick me up, if you don't mind." She sounded almost…scared. And far less sure of herself than she had a few hours earlier.

"Is something wrong? You sound upset."

She expelled a strained laugh. "You'll see when you get here."

"I'm just leaving downtown, so I'll be there in about fifteen minutes if traffic is light."

Travis pressed the end call button on his phone with no small sense of satisfaction. Mission accomplished. Now there was some hope of saving the wedding from ruin, once they'd overcome the next big obstacle—transforming Jenna into an exact copy of her polished, elegant sister.

No matter how daunting the task, it had to be done, and quickly—without any more getting distracted by sexual attraction. Travis drove back to Jenna's apartment reviewing the necessary steps in his head and trying damn hard not to be thrilled at the thought of a weekend alone with the red-headed vixen.

Before they returned to Carmel, he'd be taking her to a house among the vineyards of Napa Valley, where he'd have the privacy to school Jenna on Kathryn's life without raising any eyebrows. But for the life of him, he couldn't stop the images of other things they might do alone at the country estate from invading his thoughts.

There was the matter of the condition Jenna mentioned placing on helping him, but whatever it was, he couldn't imagine it being much of a problem. More money? He'd pay it. A new car? Consider it done. A nicer apartment? She clearly had the need for one.

The central San Francisco neighborhood where Jenna lived was an urban jungle of decrepit Victorians, tenement apartment buildings and seedy business fronts. The people who walked the streets weren't the sort who hung out at wine-tasting parties or attended charity art auctions. Rather, many looked as though their favorite forms of entertainment might get them arrested.

Travis questioned his own sanity when he found a spot on the street for the second time that day and maneuvered his Mercedes into it. His car had gathered plenty of looks as he'd driven along, and now he'd be lucky if it were still here when he returned. He activated the security system and hoped there weren't any smart car thieves around.

The door of Jenna's building was propped open with a brick, so he went inside and climbed the stairs to her apartment. After knocking on the door, he took time to note the peeling paint on the door frame, the worn hardwood floors, the dingy walls. Jenna's landlord needed to do some building maintenance, that was for sure.

After several minutes, there was still no answer, and Travis fought the sneaking feeling of panic in his gut that Jenna had changed her mind. He knocked again and waited some more. No one came.

He tried knocking harder, then heard a door open on the floor above.

"You trying to get in to see that red-haired girl?" A woman's voice called down.

Travis looked up the stairs toward the source of that voice, but all he could see was the landing, lit by what must have been a twenty-five-watt bulb.

"Um, yes," he said.

Then came the sound of footsteps, and the sight of fuzzy pink house slippers descending the stairs. Next came a red satin robe, and finally he had a full view of a small elderly woman with green curlers in her hair.

"She told me to let you in," she said, eyeing him with interest. "I'm supposed to ask what your name is."

"Travis Roth."

"Yep, you fit the description."

"Did she have somewhere to go?"

"Don't ask me what that crazy girl's up to." She put a key in the door, unlocked it, then presented the key to him.

"I'm supposed to give this to you so's you can return it to her."

Travis took the key, then stared at it in his palm, dumbfounded.

"You get finished with her," the woman said, "and I'm available right upstairs." She waggled her eyebrows at him and flashed what must have been her version of a seductive smile.

"Thanks," he said, forcing a neutral expression. "I appreciate your help." He pushed the door open and stepped inside Jenna's apartment before their encounter could get any more bizarre.

"The thing about us older women you can't get with a young one like that," she said, nodding in the direction of Jenna's apartment, "is that we know more."

"I'm sure you do."

"Honey, I could play your body like an accordion."

Travis shuddered at the image.

"Have a good night," he said as he closed and locked the door.

Turning away from it, he looked around the small room. Jenna was nowhere in sight, much as he'd expected, but the sound of running water came from behind a nearby door. Light was visible in the space between the door and the floor, so he figured Jenna had decided to take a shower.

He took in the mess that surrounded him. Either Jenna Calvert was a lousy housekeeper and a woman with violent feelings toward her sofa, or someone had trashed her place. But, if there had been a break-in, maybe even a struggle, it could have only just happened. Maybe Jenna wasn't even alive and well in the shower. An image of her murdered body being soaked in a bloody shower flashed in his mind, and he panicked.

"Jenna!" He raced to the bathroom door and flung it open.

There, behind the transparent shower curtain, was the unmistakable silhouette of Jenna's body, standing up, seemingly alive and well. He couldn't help admiring the perfect proportions, the tantalizing curve where her waist met her hips. Steam from the shower dampened his face, and he caught the scent of her shampoo, something feminine and fruity.

"Jenna? It's me, Travis."

She peeked out from the edge of the curtain and smiled. "Oh, hi. You got here faster than I thought you would."

Even the sight of her bare shoulder and her crimson hair, slicked back away from her face, aroused Travis. He'd definitely been working too hard lately, neglecting his social life, because instantly, he had a hard-on.

Cardiac arrest was the only appropriate reaction to what she did next. As Travis struggled to keep his jaw from sagging, she slid the curtain open and smiled a wicked half smile.

"Care to join me?" she asked, her tone playful, but her gaze leveled at him with a look of absolute daring.

There was simply no way not to look. He admired the full, round perfection of her damp breasts, the small pink nipples forming tight peaks; the narrow expanse of her waist; the incongruous but tantalizing triangle of blond curls at the peak of her thighs; the delicious shape of her long legs. Not a tattoo in sight. Rivulets of water formed all over her skin, and the only coherent thought Travis could form was that he wanted to lick them off.

Finally, he recovered the ability to speak. "It's a tempting offer…."

She sighed. "But you don't think it would be appropriate."

"Um…" Surely he could say something more profound than "um," but nothing came to mind.

Instead, he could only think of pinning her to the shower wall and burying himself deep inside her. To hell with propriety, to hell with everyone's expectations—he could do something wild and improper for once in his life, couldn't he?

Couldn't he?

Apparently not.

"I've shocked you speechless, I can see." She slid the shower curtain closed again. "I'll be finished in a minute, if you want to wait in the living room."

Travis closed the bathroom door, then leaned against it, barely resisting the urge to bang his head on the wall. His inability to seize the moment was so typical, so thoroughly Travis Roth, it made him want to yell.

Everything he'd accomplished in life had been through careful study and hard work. Never risk taking. His lack of daring had slowly brought the family investment firm out of a slump and into steady profitability, but as his little brother frequently pointed out, the risk takers were the ones who dominated the business world. Calculated risk, their father had always preached, was the hallmark of success. Since he'd been the man who'd built the family fortune, he had the right to preach.

And here was Travis, presented with the erotic invitation of a lifetime, and he couldn't take it. But so what? Business and personal matters weren't the same, and risk taking had entirely different kinds of repercussions for each. He wasn't going to beat himself up for not hopping into a shower with a woman he'd only just met. Getting involved sexually with Jenna would be a huge mistake anyway.

He glanced around again at the mess of her apartment, finally remembering why he'd rushed into the bathroom in the first place. At least he knew now that she was unharmed, but that didn't explain the chaos in her apartment.

Was she just the world's lousiest housekeeper? Was she mentally unstable? That could explain the shower incident, too…. Yet he had the feeling this was definitely a mess someone else had made.

On the other side of the door, the water cut off, and he heard the shower curtain slide open. Travis pushed aside thoughts of Jenna's naked, wet body and walked across the room to look at the books strewn around the bookcase. He bent and picked up some of them, placing each one on a shelf after reading the title. Classics, mysteries, biographies, romance novels, memoirs, philosophy—Jenna seemed to read it all.

He supposed he shouldn't have found that surprising, since she was a freelance journalist. That career suggested a certain intelligence and curiosity, both traits Travis had to admit he considered incongruous with her wild image.

He'd just bent to pick up a copy of the *Atlantic Monthly*—definitely not typical vixen reading material—when Jenna emerged from the bathroom dressed in a pair of faded jeans and a white sleeveless top that laced up the sides. Her damp hair had been pulled back into a sleek ponytail, and her face was scrubbed clean of makeup except for a hint of red on her lips.

Her gaze lingered on him, and rather than looking embarrassed by the shower incident, as Travis imagined he did, Jenna seemed amused.

"I guess Mrs. Lupinski let you in, no problem?"

"She offered to play me like an accordion, but yes, she let me in." He winced at the image and held out the key that was still in his hand. "Here's your key back."

"Thanks. Don't worry, my place doesn't normally look like this."

"What happened?" He was almost afraid to ask.

"While we were having lunch today, someone came in the open window and ransacked it. They stole my laptop and all my backed-up files."

A sense of outrage rose up in his chest on behalf of Jenna. "I'm sorry."

"Not as sorry as I am."

"But why would someone take all your files? Do you have other copies anywhere?"

"It's a long story, and yes, I do have some hard copies and disks of some of my work, but a lot of the newer stuff is lost. I'd hidden emergency backups in my closet, but I wasn't very methodical about backing up regularly."

"We've got a long drive ahead, so you can tell me on the way why someone would want to steal your files."

"A long drive where?"

"To Napa. My family has a country home there, a private place where we can get you up to speed on impersonating Kathryn."

"We haven't even discussed my condition for helping you yet."

Up until a few minutes ago, he'd been pretty sure whatever she wanted wouldn't be a problem, but now he knew firsthand that Jenna could be...unpredictable. Outrageous. Wild.

"Okay, let's hear it."

She stepped over a mangled couch cushion and sat on the arm of the sofa next to him. He could smell the fruity shampoo scent from her hair, and that, combined with her proximity, was intoxicating.

"First, I want to apologize for my behavior in the bathroom."

She certainly could have done worse. "Apology accepted."

"I have these sort of urges when I get stressed out."

"Urges?" He couldn't wait to hear her explanation.

"Yeah, urges." She paused, giving him a once-over. "Whenever life gets stressful, I tend to react by following my impulses, which can lead to rather outrageous behavior, as you saw in the bathroom."

Travis shrugged. "No harm done." Other than the image of her lush body burned in his memory for eternity.

"I'm getting this vibe about you."

"What sort of vibe?"

Her eyes sparked mischief. "An uptight one."

"Thanks, that's just the impression I was going for."

"You strike me as one of those guys who's going to die at an early age from a heart attack or a stroke, before you ever get to relax and enjoy life."

Travis ignored the protests of his ego and bypassed her insult. "I'm still waiting for your condition on the deal."

"That's what I'm talking about. You and I, we have a mutual need. I'm stressed out by crazy people stalking me, and you're stressed out by your job or my sister's wedding or whatever. We both need to let off some steam."

He thought of the way he'd snapped at his brother that very morning before coming to meet Jenna. Blake had simply been acting like his usual irresponsible self, turning in a report late, and even though Travis always set artificial deadlines for his brother to make sure the work really got to him when he needed it, he'd exploded right there in the office, in front of his secretary—which meant the entire office building knew about it by now.

Yeah, he definitely needed to let off some steam.

"So what does that have to do with the deal?"

"I'll impersonate Kathryn starting next week. But until then, I'm Jenna. You can coach me on acting like Kathryn, but after hours, I'm still me. All weekend long, we work on unwinding."

Travis didn't quite see where she was going, but he played along. "Okay, I've always found the wine country to be relaxing. Slower pace, quiet—"

"That's not what I mean. The most effective place I know to relieve stress—to *really* relieve it—is in bed, and I don't mean sleeping."

Travis blinked. He couldn't argue with her there. Nothing like sex to put the spring back into his step. But he hadn't even had a serious date lately, let alone—

She continued. "You're single, I'm single, we're attracted to each other, I think. No one will have to know."

"Let me get this straight. You want to make a sexual relationship part of our business agreement?"

"Not when you put it like *that*. I'm just saying I need a little companionship this weekend, and I think you do, too."

Travis frowned. A weekend alone, letting off steam, as Jenna put it, with one impossibly sexy woman. It was either the best idea he'd heard in a long time, or it was absolutely nuts.

3

JENNA SURVEYED THE apartment she'd called home for the past year, feeling yet another burst of anger at the person who'd invaded her privacy and stolen her most valued possessions. It took all her willpower not to kick something—more proof that she needed to unwind. She glanced down at the duffel bag and backpack that held everything she planned to take with her, then up at Travis Roth, who apparently was stunned silent by her proposition.

"I'm not saying I wouldn't like to…unwind," he finally said, "but don't you think it might be awkward?"

"If it is, we won't do it. Just give it a chance tonight, and if it feels wrong, we'll pretend we never had this conversation. Deal?"

If he turned her down, Jenna really was going to kick something. Namely, him. In the ass. Right out her door.

"Okay." He smiled, and the sexy gaze he pinned her with warmed her body in all the right places. "You have a deal. I'd be crazy to turn you down, after all."

She did a mental happy dance. *Look out Travis Roth, you're in for the weekend of a lifetime.*

Jenna switched off all the lights except the one near the door, then started to pick up her bags, but Travis grabbed them first. After he took them out the door, she switched off the last light and locked up her tiny apartment, with the odd feeling that when she returned, her life was going to be very, very different.

While Travis loaded her bags into the trunk of his pristine silver Mercedes, Jenna settled back into the plush gray leather of the passenger seat and tried not to think too hard about what she'd just gotten herself into. She'd focus on the fun part for tonight—do a little flirting, find out what had put all that tension into her companion's shoulders, and do her best to work it out.

It seemed her desire to focus on the positive was not to be fulfilled though. They'd barely been on the road for five minutes when Travis brought up the one subject she most wanted to forget for the weekend.

"Care to tell me why you think someone broke into your apartment and ransacked it?"

"I guess you won't leave the subject alone until I do."

"Probably not."

"I'm researching a story that someone doesn't want written. This was supposed to be the piece that established my reputation as a serious journalist."

"What's the subject?"

"An exposé on the beauty-pageant industry—on the exploitation and behind-the-scenes stuff most people don't know."

Travis nodded. "Sounds interesting. How can you be sure that's why your apartment was broken into?"

"Pretty quickly after I began researching the story, I started receiving threatening phone calls, then other strange things started happening."

"Like what?"

"I was nearly run down by a car earlier this week. It actually drove up onto the sidewalk where I was walking, and it didn't have license plates on the front or back."

His eyebrows shot up. "You don't think it was an accident?"

"An almost identical accident happened with a different car the day before."

"Who knew you were writing the article?"

Jenna pressed her fingers to her temples. Her left eye was starting to twitch, a sure sign that she was overstressed. "More than a few people. Let's talk about this another time, okay? Right now, I just want to pretend I have a normal life."

"So tell me why you and Kathryn don't speak to each other."

Yet another pleasant subject. Jenna stared out the window at the city lights passing by on the East Bay. The eye twitch was getting worse.

"I think I have a right to know what I'm dealing with here. Kathryn said she had no idea why you hated her so much, but I'm betting she wasn't telling the whole story."

"You'd win that bet."

"She has a tendency to only remember stories that make her look favorable, doesn't she?"

"Yep, that's my sis."

"So tell me your side."

"My mother used to enter my sister and I in these horrible beauty pageants all the time—Little Miss Twin California, Little Miss Twin U.S.A., Little Miss Twin America—we did the whole circuit." She scoffed. "I hated it, and Kathryn adored it. That basically sums up our differences."

"You didn't ever want to be Little Miss Twin America?"

"I hated dressing up, wearing makeup, being gawked at by crowds, the whole bit. By the time we were eight, we knew how to apply mascara flawlessly."

"Makeup on an eight-year-old?"

"You think that's young? I have photos of myself wearing lipstick at the age of three."

"So that explains your interest in the beauty-pageant story."

"I've wanted to do this story as long as I've been a journalist."

Travis nodded. "I had no idea your mother was such a…"

"Wacko? That's why I'm not exactly close to her, either."

"Wacko is not quite the word I was looking for, but if you had the kind of mother who dressed you up in matching twin outfits, why not matching names, too, like Kelly and Nelly?"

"It's almost as bad, Jenna Kathleen and Kathryn Jennifer."

"Oh." He fought a smile. "But these pageants were when you were kids, right? Why all the bad feelings after so many years?"

"That was just the beginning. Kathryn always resented me for dropping out of the pageant circuit during our freshman year in high school, thereby ruining her chances of being Miss Twin Anything. It was her big dream to win a pageant, and she never did."

"And that made your mother angry, too?"

"She never said so in so many words, but I knew she was disappointed. She always identified more with Kathryn, and by the time we were teenagers, my sister and I had an all-out rivalry going. She stole my boyfriends, my favorite sweaters and my study notes."

"So you rebelled?"

"In a big way. Where Kathryn was always Miss Perfect—at least to the outside world—I turned into the wild one. I started dating the bad boys she wouldn't dream of being caught with, wearing clothes way too sexy for her taste and I dyed my hair whatever color suited my mood."

"I have to admit, that sounds like an effective way of solving your problems with her."

Jenna smiled nostalgically. "She never once stole one of my black lace see-through tops."

"How long has it been since you've spoken to Kathryn?"

Jenna frowned, unable to immediately recall. "Maybe at a family Christmas get-together a few years ago. And even then, I doubt we said more than 'pass the turkey.'"

"That's too bad. I know Kathryn isn't the deepest person in the world, but she seems to have matured in the time she's been dating my brother. Maybe this wedding will give you a chance to reconcile with her."

Reconciling with her sister sounded about as appealing as diving into a pit of snakes, but she kept silent as she mulled over the possibility. Maybe it was time to let go of her resentment, forgive Kathryn and move on. Or maybe it was just time to get a good laugh at her sister with her new jumbo lips and chipmunk cheeks. Part of Jenna did secretly hope they remained permanently inflated.

"What about you and your brother?" she asked, not ready to discuss something as heavy as forgiveness. "Your relationship with him can't exactly be normal if you're going through all this trouble to hold his wedding together, and I remember you saying he's your father's favorite."

"Blake has never grown up. He's still a little boy playing office at our family business, and our clients can tell."

"So you have to cover for him?"

"In his business life only, up until now."

"You don't have to go around covering for my sister's mistakes, too, you know."

"If I want this wedding to go smoothly, I do." His grip seemed to tighten on the steering wheel.

Jenna stared at his profile as he drove, trying to fathom exactly how much loosening up Travis needed. Definitely more than she'd first suspected.

"What about the rest of your family—do they know what a screwup your brother is?"

"Everyone else finds his boyishness charming. Father wants him at the forefront of the company because he says Blake has the personality to win clients and keep them. He thinks I'm too stiff and serious."

"Hmm. Do you agree with him?"

"I've brought in most of our newer clients myself. When people look for someone to invest their money, they want to know they're leaving their savings in stable hands."

Stability. Why did that quality suddenly sound so sexy, when applied to Travis? Okay, so he could probably make doing a crossword puzzle look sexy, and maybe recent events were causing her to crave stability in her life, but still…

"Have you ever let things slide? Just relaxed and not worried about other people's mistakes?"

"Not when it comes to business—no."

Jenna studied his profile again. He seemed to be in deep thought, and she imagined him fantasizing about suddenly not being so responsible.

Maybe she was helping him loosen up already. She settled back into her seat and stared out the window, content with the silence after such a harrowing afternoon.

They'd been driving for almost a half hour when Jenna came out of her trance and glanced over at Travis again. His gaze dropped to the dash as they passed a sign for a town in another mile.

"We'd better stop to find some dinner and a gas station. Are you hungry?"

"Starved. I know a place at the next exit that has great ribs." She'd stopped there once with a friend on their way back to the city after a weekend hiking in the mountains.

She decided not to mention that it was a bit of a biker bar. Or that she fully intended to get Travis drunk and make him forget all about his worries for the night.

Travis followed Jenna's directions to a gravel parking lot populated with more than a few Harley-Davidson motorcycles and an even larger number of pickup trucks. The restaurant with the great ribs turned out to be a seedy-looking joint named Lola's Place, and Travis had the distinct feeling that it wasn't a restaurant so much as it was a biker bar. The flashing Budweiser sign in the front window was further support for his suspicion.

But he gave no protest, since she was probably expecting him to refuse to go in. He felt strangely compelled to defy her expectations, whatever that might entail.

He thought to remove his sportcoat and leave it in the car, but before they entered the bar, Jenna gave him a once-over and shook her head. Without so much as asking, she began unbuttoning his shirt cuffs and loosely rolling up his sleeves. After she'd done that, she reached up and mussed his hair a bit, then nodded her approval.

"Wouldn't want you to stand out too much," she said with a little smile.

Then she took his hand and led him inside. Travis was amazed at the way she took charge. He couldn't remember the last time a woman had dared to assert her will on him. His dates were always so careful, so appropriate, so obviously trying to impress him with their polish and impeccable manners. They were even polite in bed.

He'd pretty much given up on dating in the past year. It seemed a futile effort, since he attracted nothing but gold diggers. And one thing he wanted to be sure of before he ever got serious about a woman was that she wasn't marrying him for his money. Short of disguising himself as a janitor, he wasn't sure how to find a woman who really wanted him and not his family fortune.

Inside the dimly lit bar, they found a booth near the dance floor and sat down, gathering quite a few stares along the way. Travis surveyed the crowd and decided that even with his sportcoat abandoned and his sleeves rolled up, he stood out.

The menu consisted of ribs, chili, nachos and French fries, so they both ordered the ribs when a waitress showed up at their table. Just as Travis was about to ask about the selection of imported beers, Jenna ordered a Sam Adams for each of them.

"Was I about to embarrass myself?" he asked.

She smiled. "We'll never know now."

"Is this bar part of your effort to loosen me up?"

"Maybe."

"Am I going to get any direct answers to my questions tonight?"

She laughed. "If you ask me to dance, I'll say yes."

Travis glanced out at the empty dance floor. "Right now?"

"Sure. Or later, if you'd prefer."

"I'm not much of a dancer."

"Then later, after you've had a few more drinks." Her eyes crinkled with amusement.

"That beer is going to be my first and last drink. Remember, I'm driving."

Jenna shrugged. "I can drive, and I don't need alcohol to loosen up."

"What makes you think I do?"

"Just a guess."

And a correct one. Not that Travis usually drank more than a glass of wine with dinner or a scotch on the rocks with friends, but the few times he'd ever really forgotten his inhibitions, alcohol had been involved. Still, he didn't plan on admitting to Jenna that she was right.

Nor did he plan on getting drunk and acting like a fool in the middle of a biker bar.

"If I were drunk enough to get on that dance floor, what makes you think I'd be able to give you directions to our destination?"

"Hmm, you've got me there. Guess you'll just have to dance with me without the aid of alcohol."

The waitress arrived with their drinks, relieving Travis of the burden of continuing a no-win conversation. He took a long drink of his beer and decided he'd do his best to relax and have fun. After all, how often did he have the chance to spend an evening out with a woman as gorgeous and interesting and carefree as Jenna Calvert?

"Tell me more about your journalism career," he said, genuinely interested.

Jenna picked at the label on her beer bottle. "What did Kathryn tell you?"

"Just that you write for women's magazines."

"Ah, the cleaned-up version. Actually, so far I've specialized in sexual issues for women's magazines. I write those articles with titles like 'Sex Secrets of a Dating Diva' and 'Everything He Wishes You Knew about His Body.'"

"You must be fun in bed," Travis blurted and immediately regretted it. Still, he couldn't help wondering....

With a slight smile, she studied him. "I've had some good reviews."

"For your writing or your skill in bed?" What could he say—she brought out the devil in him.

"Both."

And, to think he actually had the opportunity to find out. Amazing. He had a hunch Jenna would be anything but polite between the sheets.

He forced his mind back to the present. "So are you giving up the sex articles for hard-hitting journalism?"

"Maybe. The beauty-pageant piece is supposed to be my chance to get some real recognition. I like the sex pieces, but I'm running out of angles. There are only so many aspects of it to write about."

"Do you already have a publisher for the story?"

She nodded. "*Chloe* magazine paid me an advance for it, but if I can't recover my research and get the article written, I'll have to pay it back."

"Do you still want to write it?"

"I'd like to sound brave, but lately I've been thinking maybe it's not worth getting run over by a car for."

He felt a protective impulse surge in his chest. He generally didn't have urges to fight, but if he could get hold of the person or people who'd tried to harm Jenna, he'd like to give them a thorough pounding.

Instead, he lamely offered, "Surely the police can track down whoever is responsible for harassing you."

Jenna took a long drink of her beer. When she plunked it back down on the table, Travis caught a mischievous glint in her eyes. "How about you take me out on the dance floor now and help me forget all about my career problems?"

"I think our dinner will be here soon. Maybe after—"

She stood and grabbed his hand, then pulled him up from the booth. Before he could offer a protest, she had him on the dance floor, which was now populated with a few couples. The juke-box was playing a bluesy rock song he didn't recognize.

Then Jenna started to dance, and he was mes-merized. He had some vague recollection of mov-ing his body to the music as he watched her hips sway and her torso twist, her long, heavy pony-tail draped over one breast.

When her arms snaked around him and urged his hips to move in time with hers, his body came alive in a way that he was pretty sure it hadn't since high school.

He'd just started to appreciate dancing in a whole new way when he felt a tap on his shoul-der. Travis turned to find a large bald guy with a tattoo of a snake twisting around his bulging left bicep glaring at him.

"My turn to dance with the lady," Tattoo Guy said.

Why was this bad movie scene happening to him?

"Sorry, she's with me," Travis said, making an effort to keep his voice assertive but neutral.

He turned back to Jenna, whose expression had grown wary.

A large hand grasped his shoulder and tugged him backward. "I *said* I want to dance with the lady."

Tattoo Guy inserted himself between Travis and Jenna, though Travis only needed to take a glance at Jenna's expression to guess that she wasn't going for the new dance arrangement.

When the guy tried to slip his hands around her waist, she took a step back. "Back off! I don't want to dance with you."

Travis stepped between them again. "The lady has made her wishes clear. Now if you'll please—"

He didn't have time to finish his sentence before a fist came barreling into his stomach, and the next sound he heard himself utter was an "umph" as the air left his lungs and pain pierced his gut.

Bringing to mind every lesson he'd learned from watching boxing, Travis ducked to avoid the next punch, then did his best Muhammad Ali impression on Tattoo Guy.

He heard Jenna screech for help from somewhere nearby, and a moment later he and his opponent were scrambling on the ground. Then someone was pulling him up and a burly guy in a leather jacket was picking his opponent up off the ground and dragging him toward the door.

Jenna pushed through the sudden crowd on the dance floor to his side. "Are you okay?"

"I'm fine," he said, though his insides were feeling a bit off-kilter.

A large-hipped platinum blonde wearing a Lola's Place T-shirt approached them. "Sorry about that," she said. "Reuben's a troublemaker I should have banned from here a long time ago."

"It's okay, no harm done."

She extended her hand to him. "I'm Lola, and your dinner and drinks will be on the house tonight, to make up for your trouble."

Travis looked at Jenna to gauge whether she actually wanted to stay. She shrugged and thanked Lola, then took Travis's hand and led him back to the table. Again he had the distinct sensation of every eye in the place following them.

They sat back down at the table where their ribs and fries were already waiting.

"You probably don't have much of an appetite," Jenna said.

Considering that several of his internal organs had just been pounded, Travis probably shouldn't have felt like wolfing down the rack of ribs on his plate, but suddenly he was ravenous. He had the urge to go out and hunt for something, haul it back to the fire over his shoulder and eat the charred meat right off the bone.

"Travis, are you okay?"

Jenna slid her hand across the table and grasped his.

"I'm fine."

"You just look a little wild-eyed."

"I guess it's the adrenaline."

"Thank you for defending me. It's been a long

time since a guy has put himself in danger to protect my honor."

And after he ate the meat he'd bagged himself, he wanted to take his woman back to the cave and—

Whoa. Where was all this caveman stuff coming from?

"You're welcome, but it was nothing."

He turned his attention to the ribs and dug in. Neither of their appetites seemed to have been harmed by Reuben the Tattoo Guy, and by the time they finished their dinner, Travis had nearly forgotten he was sitting in a biker bar. He'd also managed to relax and almost forget that his association with Jenna was a bizarre arrangement necessitated by her sister's botched face enhancements. Their conversation faded into an easy silence marked by occasional small talk of the sort he usually only engaged in with longtime friends.

When they left the bar and walked out into the cool night air, it seemed perfectly natural to slip his arm around Jenna's waist and guide her to the car. She stopped at the passenger door and turned to face him, putting their bodies in close contact.

He recognized the wicked gleam in her eyes.

"Now that we've danced and had dinner, there's only one logical next step," she said as her hand wrapped around his neck and into his hair.

He absolutely could not resist the urge to lean his weight into her, pressing her against the car. Their bodies fit together too perfectly for it to be a coincidence.

"What's that?" he whispered, but he already knew.

"Kiss me," she said, and he was there as soon as the words left her mouth.

4

JENNA KISSED LIKE a woman on a mission. Her
tongue caressed Travis's lips, then slipped inside
his mouth, and a moment later he felt her hands
gripping his buttocks, pressing him into her as
she snaked one leg around his. Her enthusiasm
was just as intoxicating as the rest of her.

Travis's pulse raced, and he returned her hunger with his own, deepening the kiss as one hand
held the back of her head and the other slid up her
rib cage. When she began to suck on his tongue,
he found his thoughts moving into X-rated territory, wondering what other parts of him she might
toy with so provocatively.

His hand inched upward and cupped her
breast, which was just as full and lush in his palm
as he'd imagined. With his erection straining
against her, his entire body on fire, he wondered
how the hell he'd manage to drive the rest of the
way to Napa without pulling off to the side of the
road and taking her in the passenger seat.

When they came up for air, Jenna's lips were
swollen and her eyes half-lidded as she smiled up
at him.

"Are you feeling relaxed yet?" she asked.

"Far from it."

"Guess I'll have to try a little harder then."

"If you try any harder, the last thing I'll be is relaxed."

She bit her lower lip, then slowly released it and sighed. "We'd better be going, hmm?"

Going where? Oh, right, to the country house. Travis tore his gaze away from Jenna and surveyed the parking lot, idly wondering where the nearest hotel was. A couple climbing aboard a black motorcycle eyed them with interest. He spotted the gas station lit up across the street and remembered that they needed to fill up.

"Yeah, we'd better. I think we're still a half hour away." But if they happened to pass a hotel along the way, he wasn't sure he'd be able to keep himself from screeching into the lot and dragging Jenna to the nearest available room.

An image of making love to her on a cheap bedspread in a sleazy motel room flashed in his mind, and he banished it. How had he so quickly gone from respectable businessman to crazed guy who got into bar fights and fantasized about frenzied motel sex?

He looked back at Jenna, and he knew in an instant. Reluctantly, he peeled himself off of her, and they got into the car.

They drove to the gas station, and Jenna said something about buying some weekend reading material before disappearing into the twenty-four-hour convenience store. Travis watched her moving through the fluorescent-lit store, unable to tear his gaze from her as he pumped gas and then used his credit card to pay at the pump.

When she came back out, Jenna flashed a wicked smile at him before she got back into the car. As he was pulling out of the lot, she produced an issue of *Cosmopolitan* from the bag.

"This caught my eye," she said as she read the cover. "'The All-Sex Issue. Ten fun erotic quizzes to share with your guy.'"

Travis felt his mouth go dry. Erotic quizzes? He was in even bigger trouble than he'd thought.

"Mind if I use the reading light while you're driving?"

"Go ahead. You're not going to quiz me while I'm driving, are you?"

"Don't worry, these are no-brainer questions—all in good fun. They might even help you relax."

"That's doubtful."

He heard pages being flipped through as he got back on the highway headed toward Napa Valley. When he glanced over at Jenna and spotted the curve of her breast in the skimpy white shirt, her nipples slightly erect, his groin stirred all over again.

The last thing he needed was an erotic quiz. No, he needed a cold shower and a stiff drink. Not that he was a prude—he just wasn't altogether sure he was cut out for a casual, no-strings-attached sexual fling with a woman he barely knew. Even worse, she was the sister of his soon-to-be sister-in-law, which meant they'd be bound together by family in a matter of weeks.

Travis liked his sex hot, but he kept it restricted to uncomplicated relationships, even if they had been few and far between recently.

Jenna, though… Her effect on him was impossible to ignore, maybe even impossible to resist. Just this once, he was willing to let propriety fall by the wayside and see what happened. Hell, maybe he would even find himself refreshed and relaxed as she said, ready to face the world again with renewed energy after this weekend was through.

"Ooh, here's a good one. 'Intimate Questions for Intimate Fun,'" Jenna said. "Make sure you answer these as honestly as possible. No editing your responses to suit what you think is the right thing to say."

Okay, so what did he have to lose? Besides his self-respect?

"You'll be answering them, too, right?"

"You answer the first quiz, and I'll do the next."

"That hardly seems fair."

"You choose the quiz I have to do, okay?"

"I'm driving."

"I'll read them aloud to you."

"I'm not going to win this argument, am I?"

"Not likely. Question one," she said, declaring herself the victor. "'What's your wildest sexual fantasy?'"

She was sitting right next to him, but Travis decided it would be better not to admit that. "Do I have to answer this?"

"No, but what's it going to hurt? Have you ever had sex with a woman who knew your most intimate fantasies?"

"I don't think so."

"Sex is hotter when your inhibitions are gone. If you tell all from the start, what inhibitions could you have left?"

"Okay, wildest sexual fantasy…" He had a feeling he was about to reveal himself as a meat-and-potatoes kind of guy when it came to sex. "I guess I've always had this fantasy about having sex with a stranger on a cross-country train."

"Oh, the old train scenario."

"You mean it's a common fantasy?"

"Right up there with airplane sex."

She stretched out her long legs, and Travis recalled the feel of her leg snaked around his, which led to an image of both her legs, naked and wrapped around his hips. He gripped the steering wheel tighter and glared straight ahead at the road.

"So if I have a common fantasy, does that mean I'm a boring lover?"

"No, it just means you have a conventional fantasy life. I'll bet you're anything but boring."

"Based on what?"

"The way you kissed me in the parking lot."

Oh, that. Just the mention of it set his blood

boiling again, and he caught himself scanning the horizon for motel signs.

Something had to give.

"I've never had any complaints," he felt compelled to add, then felt foolish for trying to boost his own image.

"Question two. 'What's the most scandalous place you've ever made love?'"

Travis flipped through sexual encounters in his memory—bed, bed, bed, bed... Okay, so his love life was a bit predictable. "The back seat of my father's Jaguar after the prom?"

Silence.

Travis glanced over to see Jenna's expression. She was staring at him with a look of...pity? Great, he was worse off than he thought.

"What?" he demanded, glaring at the road again.

"We'll fix that."

"I wasn't aware that I needed fixing."

"Not you, just your sense of adventure."

"So what's the wildest place *you've* ever done it?"

"I'm asking the questions here," Jenna said.

"Afraid to tell me?"

"No, I just don't want to ruin my air of mystery."

"I've ruined mine."

"I'm not telling."

"Then I'm not answering any more of these ridiculous quiz questions."

"If you think these are ridiculous, then you'd better not read my recent article, 'What Your Favorite Sexual Position Says about You.'"

Travis bit his lip to keep from smiling. "How, exactly, did you go about researching that?"

"Sadly, the research wasn't as hands-on as you might imagine. I mainly interviewed sex and relationship experts. But I learned a lot, and I bet I can guess your favorite position."

Travis tried to imagine himself having this conversation with any of his previous girlfriends. They'd all been comfortable discussing stock options, European vacations, who among their mutual acquaintances had most recently acquired the most impressive car or house…. But favorite sexual positions?

Never.

"I admit, I'm intrigued. What's my favorite position?"

"Girl on top, of course."

Travis pretended to be intently focused on the highway ahead. "What makes you say that?"

"Guys like you, who are always in charge, always responsible for things outside the bedroom, often like to give up control between the sheets."

"You seem awfully confident that you've got me sized up."

"I'm a pretty good judge of these things," she said, sounding supremely satisfied with herself.

Travis had to admire her confidence. Even if she didn't know him from Adam, she put up a good front. "I'll let you believe what you want."

"Okay then, next question—"

"No more quiz questions right now. I'm having trouble driving and talking about sex at the same time."

"That's okay. I can understand your not wanting to reveal your insecurities to me so quickly." He could hear the playful taunting in her voice, and he found it inexplicably sexy.

"What do these sex questions have to do with my hypothetical insecurities?"

"They're never more apparent than when sex is the topic of discussion."

"Ah, I see. You've been reading too many of these fluffy women's magazines."

"Hey, I write for these fluffy women's magazines."

"Oh, that's right. Do you have any articles in that issue?" he asked, knowing he was going to feel like a real ass if she said yes.

"As a matter of fact, I do. 'Ten Ways to Keep Him Begging for More.'"

He doubted she even had to do any research for that one. Jenna seemed to be a woman who knew her own sexual power. One kiss and she nearly had him begging for more.

He shifted in his seat and adjusted his grip on the steering wheel. "Do I dare ask about the content of that one?"

"*Do* you dare? I'm thinking a weekend-long hands-on demonstration is called for."

Demonstrate away, baby. "If you insist," he said, a slow smile spreading across his face. "I'm looking forward to it."

Understatement of the decade. If he didn't get a grip, he was going to completely lose sight of why he'd hired Jenna in the first place. He had to remember: business first, pleasure second. And that shouldn't have been difficult, since it was basically the philosophy by which he'd lived his entire life up until now.

Up until now.

Damn if he wasn't itching for a change.

JENNA SURVEYED the grounds of the Roth family's "country house" and expelled a sigh of appreciation. Even in the darkness, she could see that the property had a prime location among the vineyards. The well-manicured lawn led up to an imposing estate that seemed a bit extravagant for a so-called vacation home, and the hint of hills she could see spreading out into the distance suggested beautiful views in the daylight.

Then she turned to see Travis removing her bags from the trunk, and she experienced an entirely different kind of appreciation. He was a stunning male specimen. Ever since their kiss in the biker bar parking lot, her body had been on fire, her senses hyper-alert. She couldn't remember the last time she'd wanted a man so badly.

And teasing him in the car with the magazine quiz had gotten her far more hot and bothered than she'd expected. Something inside her was driven to push his limits. It was that mussing-up impulse again, only now more than a few hours ago, she had an idea of just how much mussing he needed.

But this estate—whoa.

It served as a reminder of the wide gulf that separated them. Guys like Travis and girls like Jenna didn't get together. Not in real life, not unless girls like Jenna were career social climbers, which she wasn't. And she didn't want to be mistaken for one, either. It occurred to her for the first time that maybe her little erotic stress plan could be seen by Travis as an attempt to get her hooks into his wallet via whatever means necessary.

That couldn't have been further from the truth, but she had no idea how to broach the subject. When he locked the car and carried the bags to where she stood on the sidewalk, she decided straightforward was the best approach.

He nodded at the house. "So what do you think?"

"It's beautiful, but there's one matter we should address before we engage in any, um, stress relief."

"Sure." His gaze searched her, and then he said, "Why don't we get you settled in your room first, then talk?"

Jenna followed him into the house, along the way admiring the grand entryway with its Spanish tile work and high ceilings. The house was dark, so Travis switched on lights along the way, pointing out rooms as they went.

"Over there is the formal living room and the library. In the back you'll find the kitchen, and up here," he said, as they began to climb the stairs, "are all the bedrooms."

He led her down a hallway with walnut floors, the walls lined with photos of distinctly similar-looking people who, Jenna assumed, were various members of the Roth family, and then he stopped at a door on the left at the end of the hall. She resisted the urge to stare at the pictures and hurried to catch up.

"I thought you might like this room," he said as he opened the door and switched on the light. "It's the one female guests tend to use."

Jenna stepped inside and took in the antique black-walnut furniture, the inviting decor of red-and-pink stripes and prints, the double doors leading to the second-floor balcony.

"Wow, this is beautiful," she said as she went to the door and looked out at the sprinkling of lights in the distance.

"The bathroom is over there," he said, nodding toward a closed door. "I'm going to make myself a drink. Would you like something?"

Jenna raised an eyebrow at him. "I thought you didn't need alcohol to loosen up."

"Trust me, a glass of wine won't do much more than make me drowsy."

"I'd love a glass, actually."

"If you follow the downstairs hallway to the rear of the house, you'll find the back door to the pool area. I'll meet you out there once you've had a chance to settle in."

She watched him leave the room and couldn't help thinking the drinks were an excuse to get as far away from Jenna's bed as possible. She could tell he was more attracted to her than he wanted to be. The heat they'd generated with their kiss earlier had been scorching. Jenna would have bet he wasn't accustomed to such chemistry.

On the other hand, *she* wasn't accustomed to lusting after high-society hotties.

Jenna turned and eyed her grungy old bags, looking forlorn against their elegant backdrop. She dug out her toiletries and cosmetics, then took them to the bathroom. It turned out to be four times the size of her little bathroom at home, complete with jetted bathtub, a separate stand-up shower and a gigantic vanity with a dainty padded stool for leisurely beauty routines.

She placed her drugstore cosmetics on the marble countertop and gave herself a once-over in the mirror. Her hair was still damp from the shower earlier, but it was so thick it might stay damp for days if she didn't release it from the ponytail to let it air-dry. After pulling out the hair band, she ran her fingers through the tangles and surveyed the results.

Her hair was naturally wavy, and it tumbled over her shoulders and down over her breasts in a riot of burgundy waves. Perfect for seduction. Her lipstick was gone now, but she knew that most men liked the fresh-from-the-shower look just as much as they liked a woman with a perfect makeup job, so she opted to leave herself bare.

She wandered back downstairs and through the house until she found a large living room with doors that led out to a veranda, where she could see lights on and Travis sitting at a wrought-iron patio table, sipping a glass of red wine.

When he heard her open the door, he looked over and smiled. "I thought you might like a medium red. It's from the family vineyard."

Jenna sat down across from him and looked out at the pool, a brilliant azure blue lit up in the night. "Thanks." She took a sip and let the vaguely fruity, spicy flavor settle on her tongue. "It's nice."

"What do you want to talk about?"

"This house—it just reminds me that you and I, we aren't exactly a likely pair for falling into bed together."

His smooth, strong forehead creased. "I'm not following you."

"I want you to understand that I have no interest in you for your money. Whatever happens between us this weekend—it's purely sexual. You've got needs, I've got needs, and I picked up a box of condoms at the gas station. This is all about sex, okay?"

"I didn't think you were gold digging, if that's what you're afraid of."

"Good. Because I'm not. When this weekend is over, we'll go our separate ways—at least as well as we can until Kathryn shows up again. Deal?"

He hesitated. "Deal."

"Good." Jenna downed the rest of her wine, then smiled at him as she placed the empty glass back on the table. "Have you ever gone skinny-dipping?"

"Does a hot tub count?"

"Yes, if it's outdoors."

"Hmm. I guess I'd still have to say no, then."

"Is there a hot tub here?"

He nodded toward the west side of the house. "In that gazebo over there. I took the cover off and turned it on in case you want to use it later."

Interesting. Very interesting.

The night air wasn't cold, but it wasn't quite warm enough to justify a dip in the pool. A hot tub sounded like the perfect skinny-dipping solution.

"Later? How about now?"

A smile played on Travis's lips. "I'm not finished with my wine."

"Bring it with you." Jenna grabbed the bottle from the table, along with her empty glass.

She started toward the gazebo without looking back. If he didn't have the sense to follow her, she had other ways of enticing him. When she reached the gazebo, she could hear the bubbling water. The inside of the hot tub was lit up, providing just enough light to illuminate the benches and walkway that encircled it.

Jenna found a small table beside the hot tub and placed the wine and glass on it, then withdrew the condoms she'd stuck in her pocket before leaving her bedroom and put those on the table, too.

She hadn't heard any footsteps yet, so she pulled her shirt over her head and tossed it aside onto a bench. Next came her sandals, then her jeans, tugged down over her hips as seductively as she could manage. She kept her back to Travis, but she knew without a doubt that he was enjoying a view of her rear end in white thong panties.

She reached behind her back and unsnapped her matching white lace bra, then tossed it on top of the growing pile of clothes. Last came her panties, which she took her time sliding down over her hips, down her thighs, taking care to bend over enough to give Travis a glimpse of pleasures to come.

As she stepped into the water, she looked over at him. He was standing up from the table, his glass of wine forgotten. She sank into the water, and he came toward her. She kept her gaze locked on him, suggesting with a little smile that she was enjoying the game as much as he was.

His own expression could be described as nothing short of hungry. He wanted her, and she'd offered him a dish he couldn't refuse. She settled back against the side of the tub, her breasts just under the water, her entire body below the surface enveloped in the water's delicious, bubbling heat.

Her nipples went rock hard when he began to unbutton his shirt, and her insides heated up to the boiling point. How she'd gotten herself into this situation with a gorgeous man she'd just met had to be a testament to the current level of stress in her life. Surely, after a weekend of sexual abandon, she'd come to her senses again.

"You've got a way with convincing people, don't you?"

"I've been called resourceful," she answered, intending to sound flip, but instead her voice was strained and a little uncertain.

He shrugged off his shirt and tossed it beside her own pile of clothes. When he removed his T-shirt to reveal a chest and abdomen so perfectly proportioned, so well sculpted Michelangelo could have taken credit for the work, Jenna's mouth went dry. She suddenly needed a drink of wine like she needed air to breathe. As he undid his belt buckle, she poured herself a glass.

When she looked back up, she saw that his navy-blue boxers did nothing to conceal an impressive erection, and as he rid himself of the rest of his clothing, she couldn't tear her gaze away again. In a matter of moments, he was gloriously naked, climbing into the hot, bubbling water.

Jenna's heart raced as she watched him. With his lean, muscular athlete's body and his penetrating eyes, Travis was far more than she'd bargained for. She felt as if it was her first time, and all her former bravado seemed to have drained away. She sat frozen, gripping the stem of her wineglass.

He settled in beside her and took the glass from her hands. "Is something wrong?"

Jenna forced a smile. "I wasn't expecting to be so attracted to you."

"Same here. You're a hell of a lot sexier than your sister."

He watched her as he took a sip of the wine, and his gaze had a warming effect. Jenna found her confidence again. Here she was, in a hot tub on a beautiful night, in a gorgeous setting, with the hottest guy she'd met in a long time. She would not waste this opportunity.

Instead, she got up onto her knees and straddled him, the damp skin of her torso growing cool in the night air. He started to set the glass aside, but she took it.

"There's more than one way to enjoy a good glass of wine," she whispered as she arched her back and poured the wine over her naked breasts.

He must have agreed with her, because he made no comment. Instead, he slid his hands around her waist and pulled her against him, taking her left breast into his mouth. She gasped as he sucked the sensitive flesh of one breast, then the other. He licked the wine from her chest, then her belly, and his hands moved down to cup her bottom.

The sensation of his fingertips, so close to ground zero, was almost more than she could take. She lifted his face from her belly and dipped her head down to give him a long, hungry kiss as a breeze picked up, but she couldn't be sure if the gooseflesh that appeared on her skin was from the night air or his touch.

When he tugged her hips down onto his lap, letting his erection strain against the sensitive flesh between her legs, Jenna couldn't resist grinding against him, rocking her hips to simulate what they really wanted. But he was oh-so-close to slipping inside her; it was too dangerous a game with a man she barely knew. She backed off and slid her hand down between them to grasp his erection.

He closed his eyes and let his head fall back as she massaged him in a slow, steady rhythm. All the while, his hands explored her, filling her with a building sense of urgency.

When she was sure she couldn't take another moment of waiting, he reached down and stilled her hand. "No fast finishes tonight," he said with a little half smile.

"Would you like some more wine?"

"There are other things I'd like more," he said as he trailed his fingertips lightly up her rib cage, along the underside of her breasts. "But wine would be nice, too."

Jenna reached for the bottle and offered him her breast as she began to pour. The wine trickled down over her flesh as he caught her nipple in his mouth along with the crimson liquid. When she'd emptied the bottle, she set it aside again and plunged her fingers into Travis's hair as he tasted every inch of flesh that had been touched by the wine.

He tugged her down against his erection again and said, "You're not trying to get me drunk and have your way with me, are you?"

"I thought it was pretty obvious."

"Getting me drunk is unnecessary," he said as he brushed a strand of hair out of her face.

"Does that mean I can have my way with you now?"

The rich, fermented scent of the wine rose up from her skin and from the hot tub. Jenna never would have considered the smell of wine one of her favorite scents until that moment.

"Only if I get to have my way with you, too."

She reached for a condom and tore open the package, then slipped the condom on Travis. When she positioned herself over him, with his head straining against her, she knew they were at the point of no return.

Consequences be damned, she was about to have sex with a man she should have been keeping a safe, wide distance from, and she was about to add yet one more item to the list of crazy stunts she'd pulled when the going got tough. But given the fact that she could already barely remember what had gotten her so stressed out in the first place, Jenna decided her strategy was a sound one.

She needed this, and so did Travis.

She shifted her hips, and he slid inside of her with one long, delicious thrust.

5

Travis watched the transformation on Jenna's face as he began to move inside her. Her eyes half-lidded, her lips parted as she emitted soft gasping sounds, she grew more lost in the motions of their bodies with each thrust. Gripping her hips, he let go of all his reservations and gave himself up to desire.

Sweet heaven, she felt too good to be real. She was his every adolescent and adult fantasy, all rolled into one irresistible package, here for his taking tonight and all weekend. Travis slid his hands up her torso, over her rib cage to her breasts, savoring the lush weight of them as he built momentum with each slow, deliberate thrust.

Unbelievable.

He wanted to take his time, to commit every sensation to memory, to be sure that when he went back to his boringly cautious life, he'd have this one wild weekend to recall, to remind himself that he was indeed alive.

The hot-tub water bubbled up around them, slapping against their skin as they rocked in unison, and Travis tweaked Jenna's erect nipples into even-tighter peaks until she leaned forward and offered one up to him. He took her into his mouth greedily, like a starving man, tasting and sucking each breast in turn until the lovemaking sounds she made nearly caused him to come too soon.

He pulled back and willed himself to regain control of his body. Then Jenna dipped her mouth to his and their moans mingled together as they made love with their tongues. After a few moments, she broke the kiss and whispered into his ear.

"You *do* like girls on top, don't you?"

"I like you on top, yeah."

"So I was right," she said, and he drove himself deeper inside her, hoping a little distraction would end the conversation.

"Hardly. I have lots of other favorite positions."

"Lots?"

Travis stilled himself. "Yeah, lots."

"Like what?"

"I could demonstrate."

"Absolutely," she said, sounding breathless. "We've got all weekend for demonstrations."

Reluctantly, he pulled out and grasped Jenna's hips, then lifted her onto the edge of the hot tub. "Is the air too cool?"

"Not as long as we keep heating it up, no."

"This is another one of my favorites," he said as he braced his knees on the steps of the hot tub and positioned himself between her legs.

A moment later, he was buried inside her again. She shifted her hips to better accommodate him and wrapped her legs around him. Leaning back on her hands, her breasts thrust up toward him, her head lolling back as she closed her eyes, she was a visual feast. Travis took in the sight of her and knew that he wouldn't last much longer, knew that he needed to have this fast and frenzied encounter, that he could then make the next one last long enough to be truly savored.

The spiral of tension coiling inside him, he pumped himself into her faster and faster. Caveman sounds erupted from his throat, sounds he could hardly recognize as his own. He'd turned from a respectable businessman into a sex-crazed animal, and he was driven by the single-minded goal of spilling himself into Jenna.

She was his sexual conquest, the catalyst for his transformation into a more primitive kind of man. He slid his hand down between them and caressed her clit with his thumb, until her quakes and gasps alerted him that she was as close as he was to release.

And then, when he could last no longer, he sent her over the edge. She clutched her legs tight around him and cried out as the orgasm coursed through her. The feel of her climax around him sent him over the edge, too. He grasped her hips tightly and succumbed to the final few thrusts as he spilled himself, giving over his very male essence to Jenna's power.

He heard himself cry out in one last caveman groan, and then they were kissing desperately, as if they'd only just found one another.

Jenna slid her hands around his neck and whispered, "That's one of my favorite positions, too."

"So you don't have one favorite, either?"

"That's for me to know and you to find out."

"Is that a challenge?"

"It's a promise."

"I'm beginning to like your promises."

Travis pulled her back into the water and onto his lap. The water bubbled up to their chests, and Jenna's still-erect nipples beckoned in a way that made conversation somewhat difficult. But with his heart still pounding from climax, his body still recovering, he needed a few minutes to rest.

"I think the wind is picking up. Maybe we should take this indoors," she said.

"I don't think I could get any more blown away than I already am."

"I'm mainly concerned about catching a cold."

"Good point. We can try out the heated pool tomorrow night, if you want."

"And tonight?"

"I've got another favorite I'd like to demonstrate."

"Oh yeah?" She smiled a wicked little smile.

"We just need to find a nice flat surface...."

"Like a bed?"

"Bed, table, floor, anything will do."

"Now you're talking like a man who knows how to relax."

He pulled her closer and placed a soft kiss on the side of her neck.

Some unnamed emotion swelled inside of him. Gratitude, he decided. That's what it had to be. He was thankful that Jenna had recognized a need in him, that she'd walked into his life at a time when he needed her most, that for one unforgettable weekend, she was his for the taking.

He couldn't even recognize himself tonight as Travis Roth. He was someone altogether different. A wild man. A man ruled by his appetites and able to toss aside propriety in favor of hot, frenzied sex.

Whatever he'd turned into, even if only for the weekend, it sure as hell felt good.

JENNA OPENED HER EYES and blinked at the bright sunlight pouring through the double doors. Odd that she was in a room that looked nothing like her own. She sat up and stretched, feeling more relaxed than she had in weeks.

The fog lifted from her brain, and she smiled at the erotic details that emerged from the night before. Travis, the wine, the hot tub, the staircase, the bed. She couldn't quite remember how they'd made it up here to the bedroom, but she had distinctly pleasant memories of what had happened once they'd gotten here.

She arose from the bed and found the bathroom, where she took a quick shower and tugged on a pair of old jeans and a stretchy little black tee, all the while wondering where Travis had disappeared without saying good morning.

Jenna wandered downstairs, led by the scent of coffee and something else—burned eggs, maybe. She found her way to the kitchen and was surprised to see Travis, dressed in a pair of well-worn khakis and a faded polo shirt, along with a crisp white cooking apron. He was frowning at a cookbook, with a plateful of unidentifiable squares sitting on the counter.

"I made breakfast, but something went wrong," he said, turning his frown from the book to the burned food.

"Is that…French toast?"

"Maybe I should have tried something simpler."

"Do you cook often?"

"Never."

Jenna repressed a smile, trying not to take the gesture for more than it was. She had to admire him for trying, anyway. "So they're a little crispy. That's okay." She went to the counter and picked up the plate of French toast, then carried it to the table, which had already been set.

"You really don't have to eat those. I had the maid stock the refrigerator before we arrived."

"You have a maid for your vacation house?"

"She only comes by once a week when no one's here, more often during our vacations."

Jenna tried to imagine how much work needed to be done weekly to a house that no one lived in, then decided it was too early in the morning to be thinking about it.

Travis retrieved butter and syrup from the kitchen and brought both to the breakfast table, then sat down and surveyed his work. He gave Jenna an apologetic shrug. "Maybe this will help disguise the burned flavor."

Not likely, but Jenna couldn't remember any man ever having made French toast for her before, so she wasn't about to complain. She simply flashed him a huge smile.

"What?"

"What did I do to deserve a homemade breakfast from a guy who never cooks?"

He poured himself a cup of coffee from the pot on the table. "Last night calls for something more than scorched French toast. I'll have to make it up to you with lunch."

Last night. Memories flooded her mind, and Jenna felt herself growing warm in the cool, air-conditioned kitchen. Yes, last night had been unforgettable.

"You're going to cook again?"

"Maybe not *cook*. But I'm sure I could assemble a nice picnic lunch. There's a gorgeous path through the vineyards. I thought you might want to take a hike."

Jenna forked two slices of toast onto her plate, slathered each one with butter and drenched them in syrup, then took a bite. Not bad, except for the overpowering taste. "See, these taste fine."

"I appreciate the flattery, but it's not necessary." She watched as Travis took a tentative bite of his breakfast, grimaced and swallowed it with some effort. "You really don't have to eat this."

Jenna took another bite, ignoring the charred flavor. Living on a tight budget in such an expensive city, she'd learned to pretend that even crappy food was a treat, and she never let a meal go to waste.

"So why don't you start catching me up on the details of my sister's life?"

"Oh, right. I'd almost forgotten that's why we're here."

Jenna, too, had almost forgotten why she'd run away from San Francisco. The thought of her ransacked apartment, her stolen computer and files, the threatening note scrawled on her bathroom mirror—it was all too much. She didn't want her weekend ruined by harsh reality.

"What's wrong?" Travis asked when he saw the change in her expression.

"I was just thinking about real life. Stuff I'd rather forget right now."

"The person trying to keep you from writing that story?"

Jenna made an overzealous cut into a piece of French toast. "Let's talk about Kathryn. Fill me in."

"Okay, but you can't avoid this topic forever. I want to make sure you're not in any immediate danger."

Having someone suddenly looking out for her

safety felt good—amazingly good. It took all her willpower not to gaze at him like an adoring puppy.

Travis picked up a file folder she hadn't noticed before, lying on the other side of the table. "I took the liberty of making notes for you to study, based on what Kathryn said you'd need to know."

"Oh. Um, great." Her sister must have gotten quite a laugh out of Jenna having to study for this task as if it were an important school exam.

"We'll go over some of the highlights orally, though. For instance, you'll need to know that Kathryn quit her job at a local art gallery a few weeks ago. She wanted to leave in time for final wedding preparations."

"Couldn't she have just taken a vacation?"

"She'll be devoting her time to the women and children's shelter after the wedding."

Of course. Jenna should have guessed—abused women had always been Kathryn's pet cause, and while Jenna used to suspect it was just a pageant gimmick, she now saw that her sister's interest was quite possibly genuine. If so, it was one of her few redeeming qualities. "Is that what you'll want your wife to do, too? Devote her time to charity work?"

His eyes sparked with amusement, and he produced a charming half smile the likes of which she'd never seen before. This was a glimpse of Travis when he wasn't being a type-A personality. "I don't have even the remote prospect of a wife. Why do you ask?"

"Curiosity."

"I've never given it much thought. I wouldn't ex-pect my wife to do anything she didn't want to do."

"Good answer."

"Kathryn is also working with a personal trainer right now. I mention this because she's been pretty obsessed with it recently, working out for two hours a day to get ready for the wedding."

"Does she plan to sprint down the aisle and wrestle your brother at the altar?"

He smiled fully then, and it was a warm, bril-liant expression that lit up the room. Jenna found herself staring at his mouth, aching for a replay of last night.

"I hope not. I believe she wants to look good in her wedding dress—and on the honeymoon."

Kathryn had never had a problem staying thin, but Jenna could certainly see her sister freaking out about a five-pound weight gain and going to extreme measures to correct it.

"So does that mean I'll have to do these gruel-ing two-hour workouts? Won't her trainer notice my sudden lack of muscle tone?"

"I'm sure you can get out of the workouts, for the most part. But I have to warn you, I've heard her personal trainer is a bit of a fanatic."

"Where does Kathryn live now?"

"She had been renting an apartment in town, but last month she moved into the house she and Blake just bought."

"What? Won't your brother have his own key and be stopping by whenever he wants?"

Travis grimaced. "It's not an ideal situation, but if you've made it clear you don't want any physical contact right before the wedding, that will deter him, I hope."

"There's no way we can pull this off."

"We can, and we will. Kathryn said you switched places all the time as kids."

"Playing fool-the-teacher isn't quite the same as impersonating someone's fiancée."

"True."

"Your brother's going to know something's up."

"He might think Kathryn is behaving strangely, but you can explain it away as prewedding jitters. And I'll help you avoid him as much as possible."

Jenna took a deep breath and reminded herself of the money. She *could* do this, right?

Right.

"What about the rest of the family? You really think they'll buy the act?"

"Absolutely. They don't even know Kathryn has a twin," he offered, seeming to realize a moment too late that Jenna might not be impressed by that fact.

"Don't worry, I'd be shocked if she went around voluntarily telling people about her low-class twin sister."

Travis opened his mouth to protest, but Jenna stopped him.

"I don't have any illusions about my relationship with Kathryn, and frankly, I don't care."

"It seems like a shame to have a twin and not have a relationship with her."

Jenna shrugged. Maybe she had missed out a little, but she'd also saved herself plenty of headaches by not pursuing a relationship with her sister. "You must have a pretty close-knit family."

He smiled. "I've never really thought about it, but yeah, we stick together. How about the rest of your family? Kathryn doesn't talk about them much."

"We're bourgeois middle class—that's why she stays quiet. But no, there aren't any strong ties between us."

"I've met your parents at least once. They seemed like nice people."

"You met my mother and her latest husband. Our father skipped out when we were ten and hasn't been heard from since, and Mom's on her third husband now," she said, then took a drink of orange juice that tasted as if it had been fresh squeezed.

Glancing over at the kitchen counter, she spotted the pile of discarded orange halves. He'd *squeezed orange juice* for her? She repressed a satisfied smile.

"Do you like your stepfather?"

"We get along fine, but he's always been kind of oblivious to me. He makes my mom happy, though, so I don't have anything against him. It's my mother who drives me crazy. She doesn't approve of my lifestyle."

Travis's gaze darkened. "What lifestyle?"

"Don't worry. I'm not a lesbian dominatrix or anything. She just thinks my living alone in San Francisco and working as a freelance writer is a recipe for disaster."

It didn't escape her attention that her mother had been at least partly right. Her life *had* recently turned into a disaster, after all.

"Is this what you want most to do with your life?"

"Yes. I love writing, and I love being a journalist without the constraints of only writing for one publication."

"Then she should be happy for you. Not many people ever follow their dreams." He poked at his French toast with a fork, but didn't take a bite.

"How about you? Are you following your dreams?"

He shrugged. "I've always known I'd become a part of the family business."

"Spoken like a man with thwarted dreams."

"To be honest, I never gave much thought to whether or not it was what I wanted to do. I just did it because it was expected."

"Don't you think you should? Give it some thought, I mean?"

He let his gaze roam down to her chest and back up again, a slow grin forming on his lips. "We're supposed to be going over the details of Kathryn's life."

"How about I look over the file today, and you quiz me later?"

"Sounds fair. I'm having trouble keeping my mind on Kathryn anyway."

"Oh? Where exactly is your mind wandering?" Jenna flashed him her most scandalous look. She knew he'd enjoyed himself last night. It was the best sex she'd ever had, and she'd have been willing to bet he would say the same.

But still, great sex didn't mean much in the long run. It didn't equal mutual respect, love, commitment or any of the other things relationships were built on. There was no reason to think of her weekend with Travis as more than an extremely odd business arrangement.

Travis was looking at her as if he could read her mind. "Last night was amazing."

She smiled. "I told you sex was the great stress reliever."

"It wasn't just that. There's a strong chemistry between us."

Was there ever. "Animal lust. It's what drives the natural world."

"I wouldn't say that."

"Let's don't overanalyze it, okay?"

He shrugged. "You've got a way with a wine bottle."

"And you've got a way with your hands." And his mouth, and his hips, and his…

Jenna stood up from the table, too, eyeing the swimming pool outside. What she needed right now was a cold swim, a cold shower—anything to cool off the warming sensation that started in her belly and grew to a throbbing heat between her legs. No way would she be able to memorize all the details of Kathryn's life if all she could think about was making love to Travis Roth.

6

Travis peered out the window at Jenna. She was standing at the edge of the pool, dipping one toe in to test the water temperature. And she appeared to be about to take a swim in her bra and panties. He'd forgotten to mention to her that she might need a swimsuit on the trip.

He gripped the window frame, all too aware of how badly he wanted to race outside at that moment and make love to her right there beside the pool. And why couldn't he? What was stopping him? She'd be game for a little more stress relief, as she liked to call it.

But something just didn't feel right about the way she wrote off their attraction as mere animal lust. He didn't want to think of it that way. However, if that's what it took for her to justify a weekend fling to herself, then so be it. He could understand the need to keep an emotional distance, and if he weren't such a fool, he'd do the same.

Travis found an old pair of his swim trunks in the chest of drawers and undressed, then put them on. By the time he made it out to the pool, Jenna was swimming laps in the water, her long red hair slicked back as it had been last night in the shower.

She stopped swimming when she saw him. Holding herself up on the concrete edge, she smiled at him. "Come on in. The water's arctic cold."

"I forgot to tell the maid to turn on the water heater. I just switched it on, but it'll take a while for the pool to heat up."

"That's okay. I needed a cold dip." She pushed herself up and sat on the tile edge of the pool with her legs dangling in.

Travis couldn't help but stare at the way the skimpy fabric of her bra and panties revealed the treasures beneath. They were both black, but he could see the outline of her erect nipples, and other equally tantalizing details. Her skin had a natural warm peach tone that seemed to glow in the sunlight, and as he watched rivulets of water trail down her belly, he felt his groin stir.

"I didn't bring a swimsuit."

"Do you hear me complaining?" He smiled, then dived into the pool and swam a quick lap back and forth before coming up for air.

The brisk water took care of his budding erection but did nothing for the desire coursing through his veins. When he stopped swimming and looked at Jenna, it was like finding Lorelei perched at the edge of the pool, singing her siren song and luring him toward a deadly crash into the rocks of the Rhine River. He swam over to her and pushed himself up to sit beside her.

"I have to admit, seeing you like that is putting ideas in my head."

"What sort of ideas?"

"Bad, bad ideas."

She licked her lower lip and looked at his mouth. "My favorite kind."

"But we agreed that our stress-relief activities would be limited to after hours."

The rise and fall of her chest as she breathed was almost enough enticement to make him reach out and cup her breast in his hand. Instead, he balled his fingers into a fist.

She was still staring at his mouth. "Seems like a silly rule to me."

"So I wouldn't be making a breach of ethics by kissing you right now?"

"I'll make it easy for you," she murmured as she leaned forward and tilted her head, placing a long, soft kiss on his lips.

Travis grasped her by the torso and tugged her onto his lap, then slid his hands down to the cool, damp flesh of her bottom as she pressed herself against his erection. So much for restraint.

He was just thinking of ridding Jenna of her wet bra when a strange voice interrupted their kiss.

"Yoo-hoo! Mr. Roth, are you here?" called the voice from inside the house.

It took an agonizing moment for him to recognize that it was Ramona, the maid. Before he could remove Jenna from his lap, he heard a gasp from the veranda.

"Mr. Roth? I'm sorry, I—I didn't realize—" She was backing herself into the house again when she seemed to recognize Jenna. "Miss...*Calvert?* You changed your hair—"

There was an awkward silence as Ramona looked back and forth from Travis to Jenna. A wiry middle-aged woman who bore an odd resemblance to the Chihuahua she often brought along with her and left tied to the front of the house while she worked, the maid let her jaw sag as her expression grew more and more distressed. "Oh my! I'm very sorry to interrupt!"

Travis looked at Jenna, realizing a moment too late that Ramona thought she'd just interrupted an affair between himself and his brother's fiancée. With her eyes wide, Jenna scrambled up from his lap, and Travis went after Ramona, who'd disappeared into the house.

"Ramona? Ramona! Please wait." He found her in the foyer, about to leave. "I'd like to explain what you just saw."

"Really, Mr. Roth, there's no need. You have my word I'll never speak of this again."

He stopped himself. What would be worse? Having word leak out that he and Kathryn were having an affair, or having any news leak out that might compromise his plan to keep Blake's wedding afloat? Ramona had no reason to tell anyone about the "affair" and risk losing her job, so as much as he hated to have her think of him as a scumbag—even temporarily—he decided that was the safest option.

"I appreciate your being discreet," he forced himself to say. "Was there some reason you stopped by?"

"I just wanted to see if you needed anything—I was in a bit of a hurry when I was here yesterday."

"You did a great job, and thank you for stopping by again. We'll be fine."

She nodded, avoiding his gaze as she left. Travis stared down the hallway at the damp footprints he'd left on the way in, and as his swim trunks dripped, he ran one hand through his wet hair.

That encounter had only been a taste of awkward—and potentially disastrous—moments to come if he and Jenna continued their fooling around. As much as he hated the thought of not touching her, of not making love to her again, he had to consider that maybe that was the safest option. The most sensible one.

Travis found a couple of towels in the kitchen and used them to clean up the water from the floor, then tossed them in the laundry room before going back out to the pool.

He found Jenna stretched out in a chaise lounge, sunning herself. When she heard his footsteps, she lifted one arm to shade her eyes from the sun and looked at him. "She thought I was my sister?"

"And that we're having a torrid affair."

"But you set her straight, right?"

Travis sat down on the chaise lounge next to hers, making an effort not to let his gaze roam over her lush body. "No, I let her believe we're having an affair. I didn't see any point in explaining why I have you here."

Jenna pushed herself up in her chair and glared at him. "How could you?"

"It seemed like the safest option."

She stared at him for a few moments, then leaned back in her chair again and sighed. "This is so weird."

"It's only going to get weirder. I think we need to reconsider our deal."

"You want to back out?"

"Hell no, but will we really be able to pull off this charade if we can't keep our hands to ourselves?"

A breeze picked up from the west, and Jenna hugged herself. "I hadn't thought about it that way."

"Neither had I until Ramona caught us. I think we'll have to be careful how we behave toward each other, or else someone's going to notice our attraction."

"I guess you're right. So what do we do?"

He tried to force the words from his mouth, but they didn't want to come. *Stop having sex* was what he intended to say. Was what he should have said.

But he made the fatal mistake of letting his gaze drift down to Jenna's cleavage, accentuated by her crossed arms, and memories of licking red wine from those lush breasts came to him then.

What had happened to his newfound sense of daring? Where had the risk-taking Travis gone? He'd run for cover just as soon as things got dicey.

That was going to change.

All the problems waiting for him in Carmel—his brother's missing fiancée, his rocky investment firm, his constant family obligations—they could continue to wait until Monday. He *needed* this weekend alone with the sexiest woman he'd ever met, and he wasn't going to waste the entire time drilling Jenna on her sister's favorite foods or best friends' names.

No, he was going to accept the risk, because the immediate payoff was damn well worth it.

He smiled then, willing the tension to drain from his shoulders. "How about we just cross that bridge when we come to it? I'm sure we can handle ourselves like mature adults."

Jenna looked at him curiously. "Why the sudden change of heart?"

"I won't deny that you lying there wet in your underwear has a little to do with it."

She let her gaze travel over him, lingering at his waist, then at his thighs. When she met his eyes again, she said, "I think we've still got some tension to work out of you, anyway."

Did they ever.

"Do you feel up to that hike through the vineyards now?"

"I didn't bring any shoes that would be good for much more than a brisk walk."

"That's okay. It's not a hard trail, and if you get tired, I'll carry you."

She smiled. "Well, if you're offering to carry me… Before we go, I was wondering if you have a computer with an Internet connection here at the house."

"Can't stand to spend a full day disconnected from the world?"

"Actually, I just want to e-mail my editor to let her know what's happened with the story and why I'm taking a break from it."

"There's a DSL connection upstairs in the study, and you're welcome to use it. You still intend to write the story?"

"Yes, I do. I've decided I can't let anyone scare me away from it."

"Good. The police will catch the person who broke into your apartment, I'm sure."

"Whether they do or not, I'm writing the story. There must be even more than I've discovered if someone is trying to stop me."

A wave of protectiveness rose up in Travis's chest. He admired Jenna's determination to uncover the truth, but the possible danger to her had him worried.

"I hope you'll be careful."

"You sound like my mother."

Great. He'd managed to convey just the wrong image again. Travis watched her in silence, pondering his avoidance of risk taking. He had a thing or two to learn from this wild vixen who didn't seem to know the meaning of the word *risk*. Not for the first time, he wondered if it would really be possible for Jenna to masquerade as her much tamer sister for two entire weeks.

"Why don't you go get dressed and send your e-mail while I throw some lunch in a backpack for the hike?" He stood and offered a hand to Jenna.

She let him pull her up from the chair, and the contact of her hand in his was enough for his pulse to race. He willed his gaze away from her body as she walked into the house, and only when he was sure she'd reached the staircase did he make his way to the kitchen.

Explosive was the only way to describe the chemistry between them. He hadn't imagined what he'd be getting himself into when he agreed to Jenna's side of their deal. And for the next two nights, he refused to let caution get in the way, even if it meant getting burned.

JENNA STARED at the message on her e-mail account. The subject line read, "Want Your Files Back?" and the sender had used an address she didn't recognize. Her heart raced as she debated whether or not to open the message and possibly ruin what little bit of relaxation she'd been able to achieve since last night. Curiosity won out finally, and she double clicked on the message.

Don't think you can hide. The only way out is to drop the beauty-pageant story. I'll do whatever it takes to stop you. Oh, and you want your files back? Too damn bad.

Jenna reread the words, her stomach clenched

into a ball. Had this person been watching her when she'd left with Travis? Was it possible that they'd been followed all the way here to Napa County?

No, she was just being paranoid. But why was the beauty-pageant story dangerous enough to elicit death threats?

She closed the message and sat back in the plush leather office chair, her heart racing nearly as fast as her thoughts. Until now, her career hazards had included an occasional paper cut, possible carpal tunnel syndrome and bad eyesight from staring at a computer screen. Now she faced the possibility of death if she wrote a story she truly believed needed to be told.

Anger rose up in her chest and won out over fear. To hell with whoever had sent that message. She would not let cowardly threats stop her. She might be lying low for a couple of weeks, but that didn't mean she couldn't start reconstructing her research when she had the time, and it didn't mean she wouldn't dive back into the story head-first as soon as her obligation to Travis ended.

She opened a blank message and began typing a note to her editor, explaining why she'd been forced to leave town for a few weeks. With assurances that she had every intention of recovering her research and continuing to pursue the story, she finished the e-mail and hit the send button. That left her staring at the threatening message again.

She went to her bedroom and opened her backpack, dug around in it until she found the business card of the detective who was on her case and went back to the office to call him.

After a few rings, a familiar voice answered. "Detective McNeely."

"This is Jenna Calvert from the apartment break-in yesterday. I just got an e-mail message from my stalker."

"Did it give any new information?" His voice had perked up.

"Just confirmed that the beauty-pageant story is the one he doesn't want me to write."

"You've got my e-mail address on my card, right?"

"Yes."

"Forward the message to me. I'll see if we can track down a source. Probably not, with all the ways there are to set up an anonymous account, but it's worth a try. We might get lucky and find out we're dealing with a dumb criminal. We did find some unidentified prints in your apartment, but no matches in our database yet."

"Okay, great. I'm staying in Napa with a friend for the weekend, and then I'll be going with him to Carmel for two weeks."

"What's the best way to get in touch with you if anything turns up?"

"I've got my cell phone with me, but I keep it turned off. You can leave a message on my voice mail."

After she'd hung up with the detective, Jenna

swung around in the desk chair to find Travis standing in the doorway.

"Sorry, didn't mean to eavesdrop. I was just coming to tell you we can take off whenever you're ready."

"That was the police detective who's investigating my case."

"Did something come up?"

"Sort of. Take a look at this." She nodded at the computer and reopened the message for Travis to read.

He came into the office and leaned over her chair to see the monitor. When he'd finished reading, his expression grew dark, and he looked at Jenna.

"It sounds like this guy was watching you."

Jenna clicked the forward button and typed in the detective's e-mail address. When she'd sent the message to him, she turned back to Travis. "Maybe, or maybe the 'you can't hide' comment is just a coincidence. I'm not going to attach too much significance to it. This scumbag could be watching my apartment this weekend, noticing that I'm not coming or going from it, but that doesn't mean he knows where I am."

"We're talking about your safety. I think that's significant."

"Let's just forget about this for now, okay? I don't want it to ruin the weekend."

"We can't be certain you're safe here. If this person was watching you, that means he could have followed us here."

The sick knot in her stomach grew. This was supposed to be her temporary sanctuary, her escape from all the crap that had happened in the city—and now she had to contemplate the possibility that someone could have followed her here?

"Jenna?"

She shook herself out of a daze and blinked at Travis. "So now what?"

"I'll have a private investigator come check things out, maybe keep an eye on the place and let us know if he spots anything odd."

Jenna would be willing to bet he didn't have anyone of the Bodyguards For Less caliber in mind.

"That's a little drastic, don't you think?"

"It's nothing, and I'll feel much better knowing someone has an eye on things."

"So make the call, and then let's put this out of our heads."

Travis frowned. "I'm not going to be able to relax until I know you're safe. Maybe we shouldn't plan to leave the house until someone has come to check out the property."

She could think of worse things than being stuck inside a palatial Napa Valley estate with a gorgeous male, but she wasn't going to let irrational fear change the course of her weekend. This was her stress-relief time, and she'd done enough cowering behind locked doors already thanks to the jerk who was stalking her.

"I'm not going to sit around feeling vulnerable. I've done enough of that."

He sighed. "Is this another challenge?"

"Yeah." She smiled. "Minimum risk, maximum reward. How can you say no?"

"When you put it that way…" He flashed a smile that could melt panties. "Why don't I give my private investigator friend a call and then we can take off?"

"Now you're talking."

Jenna's thoughts immediately turned to the night before. She'd expected Travis to be a little cautious as a lover, maybe need some coaxing, but he'd caught her off guard with his enthusiasm. She felt as if she'd unleashed his inner wild man, and she couldn't wait to see what further risky business they'd find together.

She leaned back in the office chair, erotic images crowding her head, the last vestige of her stress melting away.

TRAVIS DROPPED the backpack in the shade of the tree and turned to look out over the vineyards below. They'd chosen the perfect spot to stop for lunch. Jenna stood nearby, admiring the view, as well. For the beginning of July, the weather was pleasantly mild, and they'd managed to hike several miles barely breaking a sweat. Along the way, Travis had quizzed Jenna about Kathryn's life, since she'd had a chance to look through the file on her sister before they left the house.

Now he wanted to get a taste of how well Jenna could play Kathryn.

"Okay, so now you're Kathryn and someone you don't recognize starts talking to you like you're the best of friends. What do you do?"

"Play along?"

"But how?"

"I know how to act. Sort of."

She wasn't exactly inspiring his confidence with her shaky tone of voice.

"Let's do a little mock scenario. I'll play the acquaintance, and you convince me that you're Kathryn."

"Is this really necessary?"

"You've got to do something to earn your pay this weekend." He produced a mischievous smile, and Jenna tossed him an annoyed look.

"Okay, so… I'm Kathryn. Now what?"

"Now, you act." He did his best impression of one of Kathryn's well-bred and utterly boring friends. "Kathryn, darling, you look fabulous this evening."

He watched Jenna fight off laughter at his bad female voice. Then, with a little tilt of her head, a modest half smile and a well-timed flush to her cheeks—a sort of coyness he'd never seen Jenna display—she transformed herself into her sister. "Why, thank you. You look absolutely stunning yourself," she said in Kathryn's trademark carefully enunciated tone.

"Did you see Lily Carlyle's new diamond? I heard it's a full two carats."

He watched as Jenna tried not to roll her eyes.

And then she was right back into character. "How lovely for her."

Good, noncommittal reply, and it sounded exactly like what Kathryn might say.

"And where's *your* diamond, Kathryn, dear? Too big to lug around on your finger?"

Jenna produced another coy smile. "I'm afraid I've overdone the working out a bit. My engagement ring got too big, so I'm having it resized."

Travis couldn't help being impressed. "Wow, that was good."

"She *is* my twin sister. For better or worse, I know how Kathryn thinks."

"This really is going to work," he said, feeling more hopeful than he had all weekend.

"You think so?"

"I've had my doubts, but as long as we can get you up to date on Kathryn's life, we'll pull it off."

Jenna stared out at the perfectly spaced rows of the vineyards, a slow smile spreading across her lush lips. "And if it doesn't work, do I still get paid?"

"Of course," he said, feeling a ridiculous stab of annoyance that she was most concerned about the money.

He was the one who'd offered the payment, so why should he be surprised that she wanted it? Clearly, he'd lost sight of what their arrangement was about, and it wasn't going to do him any good to lose sight again. Theirs was a business arrangement—unethical as it might be—and nothing more.

After having a lunch of wine and French bread

slathered with Brie under the shade tree, they continued their hike, managing to wander away from the trail Travis knew, until they came to a rock wall that Jenna insisted scaling, certain it would provide a shortcut back toward the house.

Foolishly, Travis had agreed, in spite of the fact that he had no idea how to rock climb, and he now had the bumps, bruises and sore muscles to show for it. He'd been so intent on proving to Jenna that he could take a risk, he'd lost his last shred of common sense somewhere about halfway up the cliff.

Back in the comfort of his bedroom, Travis closed his eyes and buried his face in the pillow, savoring the feel of Jenna's hands working the muscles of his back. "This isn't necessary, you know."

"Want me to stop?" she said.

"Hell no."

"I guess you weren't kidding when you said you didn't do a lot of rock climbing."

Travis winced when she hit a tight muscle. "I've *never* rock climbed before."

She began giggling uncontrollably and collapsed on his back.

"What's so funny?"

"That makes two of us," she said between bursts of laughter.

"You lied to me," he said in a tone of mock horror. After all, he couldn't very well be angry about a little deception when he'd let her believe he was familiar with the sport.

"I never actually said I'd done it before. I just

said I knew *how* to do it. As in, I've watched it on TV a few times."

Travis succumbed to a fit of laughter, too, then, as he pictured himself following Jenna's "expert" instructions on the side of the cliff and nearly getting himself killed. "Next time you decide to fake expertise at something, could you pick a subject that doesn't involve risking life and limb?"

"Hey, you had fun, didn't you?"

He would have had fun sitting and watching the clouds pass by with Jenna, but yeah, he'd had more fun today outside of bed than he could remember having in a long, long time.

"I had a pretty good time," he said, careful not to show too much of how he felt.

He wasn't sure why he thought he needed to be guarded around her, but he knew for a fact it wouldn't be wise to let emotion come into play with her now. Not when she was about to impersonate his soon-to-be sister-in-law for two weeks. And Jenna herself had made it clear that what she wanted from him was a purely sexual relationship, nothing more.

She sat up again and continued his massage, managing to go straight to his sorest spot. If he could stay in this bed forever with this woman, he wasn't sure he'd ever want to leave.

And yet they had to leave Monday morning. The thought ruined his good mood and brought harsh reality crashing back in on an otherwise perfect day.

"Is it my turn yet?"

Travis rolled over, simultaneously flipping Jenna onto her back. He pinned her to the bed and smiled a lazy smile. "Your turn for what?"

"A massage. You've gotten a full twenty minutes' worth."

"You timed it?"

"Only so I could make sure you don't cheat me when it's my turn."

"I never said I'd give you one, did I?"

She narrowed her eyes at him. "You can't breach massage etiquette!"

"Massage etiquette? Is there really such a thing?" He settled himself between her legs, ready for a good, long stay there. She parted her thighs in response and wrapped her legs around his. As exhausted as he was, he still felt himself stir.

"In my book there is."

"But that's probably the same book that tells you it's okay to lure unsuspecting men onto the sides of cliffs."

"It's my book. I get to decide what's in it."

Travis slid his hands under her shirt and found her erect nipples through the lace of her bra. "There's more than one way to give a massage, you know."

Jenna's breath caught in her throat as he squeezed her sensitive flesh. "I'm open to experimentation," she whispered.

"Good, because this massage will require you to take your clothes off."

She smiled. "Clothes only get in the way of a good massage anyway."

He tried to put out of his mind the fact that this was one of their few nights together—that tomorrow would be the last night. No need to ruin a good thing, but a pang shot through him nonetheless. He never wanted this weekend to end. And he wanted to capture the way Jenna made him feel and bottle it.

He removed his body from hers long enough to get her undressed, and once he'd rid her of her bra and panties, he settled back in to savor her.

"I hope you don't mind if I stretch the definition of massage a bit," he said.

Jenna tugged at his shirt. "I'm open to that, but I personally think the masseur should also be unhindered by clothing."

"I agree completely, but not quite yet." If he didn't have a barrier of clothing, he knew damn well that a slow and deliberate exploration of Jenna's body would be out of the question.

She trailed her fingertips across his buttocks and kissed him softly, making him forget for a moment why he wanted to hold out for a while.

"No fair trying to move things along at your pace."

"Oh, is that what I was doing?" she whispered, then traced his lips with her tongue.

"You're a shameless vixen, you know that?"

She smiled, and Travis knew he was in trouble. "Take off your clothes, and I'll show you exactly how shameless I can be."

Trouble, he decided, had never felt so good.

7

AFTER SPENDING a lazy Sunday exploring the Napa Valley countryside on bicycles Travis had found in the Roths' garage, then spending an even lazier evening making love and talking for hours, Jenna should have felt more relaxed than she had in years.

Instead, she was terrified.

It was Monday morning, and she sat frozen in the chair at the upscale San Francisco salon—a place Kathryn had recommended Travis bring her for "the transformation"—marveling at the odd sensation of her head feeling lighter. Not only that, but there was a breeze on her neck. She was afraid to look in the mirror.

She and Travis had left Napa Valley earlier that morning to head toward Carmel, but they'd stopped back in the city to visit the salon and do some shopping to complete her makeover. She'd already been treated to a manicure, pedicure and facial, and now that her hair had been restored to its natural blonde by a colorist, all she had to do was look in the mirror to see the haircut that would make the metamorphosis complete.

"What do you think of the fabulous new you?" The stylist, a man named Javier who had a buzz cut and wore all black, spun Jenna around in the chair and smiled triumphantly.

Jenna looked into the mirror and saw her sister. It wasn't Kathryn, though. She was looking at a reflection of herself, but gone was her long auburn hair and her makeup-free face. She blinked at the new image of herself and fought the nausea rising up in her stomach.

Her pale blond hair lay in thick, elegantly coiffed chunks around her face and jaw, and then there was nothing. No long, wild tresses draping her shoulders, because those tresses had fallen to the floor and had been efficiently swept up by a salon assistant. Makeup had transformed her into a polished china doll, a transformation Kathryn probably got up an hour early to make every day.

She was an identical twin again, all her uniqueness wiped away with a few hours at the salon. The nausea grew.

She just needed to focus on the money. She was doing it for the money. Twenty-five grand was enough to eliminate her constant feelings of financial insecurity. Her hair would grow back out. The makeup could be washed off.

This was no big deal.

Really, it wasn't.

Then why did she still feel like losing her breakfast?

"Well?" Javier was beginning to look nervous.

"It looks...great."

She heard footsteps and saw in the mirror that Travis had come back from making his business phone calls and was walking toward her, staring at her as if he were looking at a ghost. When he reached the side of her chair, he stopped and smiled at Javier.

"Could you excuse us for a minute, please?"

"Of course." The stylist disappeared, and Travis turned back to Jenna.

He stared for another moment in silence. "Amazing. You look exactly like her."

Jenna held up the photo of Kathryn with her latest haircut up next to her face. "He got the haircut right?"

"It's perfect. I'm sorry you had to have your hair cut off."

She shrugged. "It'll grow."

"I'm going to miss it."

Jenna stood up from the chair and removed the black smock she'd been given by the stylist. Her chest tightened inexplicably at Travis's comment.

"I'm sure this will just make our transition easier. No worries about keeping your hands off of a woman who looks identical to your brother's fiancée, right?"

"Except I know you're not her."

Jenna looked into the mirror again, turning her head left and right, marveling at the makeup job that reminded her all too much of her beauty-pageant days. "I might as well be."

"Why don't we get out of here? I've already paid, and I just saw a boutique down the street that looks like a place where Kathryn would shop."

A change of clothes would be the final step. She'd be able to waltz right into her sister's life and no one would be the wiser. But the closer she came to that moment, the more her mind and body rebelled at the idea.

"Maybe we should have lunch first. I'm getting hungry."

"Are you having second thoughts?"

"I've been having second thoughts since the moment I met you. Best not to linger on them, okay?"

Travis frowned but said nothing as he led the way out of the salon and into the bright sunshine. They walked side by side along the sidewalk of the upscale business district full of stores where only people with money to waste would shop. Jewelry shops, boutiques, cafés filled with uniformly well-dressed people...

They rounded a corner and Jenna spotted a women's clothing boutique on the left, an upscale designer shop whose name brought to mind Beverley Hills and Hollywood starlets. Jenna had never even bothered to set foot in one, and to know her sister shopped there regularly brought home just how far her path had diverged from Kathryn's.

Travis held the door for her, and she stepped into the artificially cool air, her sandal landing with a click on pristine white tile. A saleswoman who was nearly as tall as Travis hovered nearby. She looked as if she hadn't eaten more than a salad in weeks, and a shiny curtain of dark hair hung on her gaunt shoulders. Her name tag announced that her name was Allegra.

She produced something that Jenna guessed was supposed to be a smile and asked, "May I help you?"

"We're looking for a few things for the lady," Travis said.

Jenna wandered over to a rack of dresses, feeling a bit too much like Julia Roberts's character in *Pretty Woman,* and began scanning them for something Kathryn might choose.

"Of course. Any special occasion in mind?"

"No, just casual wear," Jenna said without giving the matter much thought. No way did she plan on squeezing herself into any of the stiff-necked wool suits Kathryn favored.

"I can set up a dressing room if you see anything you'd like to try on," she said, and Jenna nodded.

Ten minutes later they'd picked out some Kathrynesque pieces and were following Allegra to a dressing room equipped with a starkly modern bench seat, a matching clothes tree and walls of mirrors.

"If you need any assistance, just call for me," the saleswoman said before closing the door, leaving Jenna and Travis alone.

Jenna started to remove her shirt, but stopped.

"Don't you think this is an odd way to begin our hands-off pact?"

Travis repressed a smile. "Oh, right. Guess I forgot. I'll wait outside."

He made a move toward the door, and Jenna tugged her shirt the rest of the way off, then unsnapped her bra and let it fall to the floor. "Unless you want to postpone the pact by a few hours."

Travis's gaze dropped to her bare breasts and moved slowly back up to meet her eyes. "You love to play the temptress, don't you?"

"You're such an easy target, I can't resist."

"I should feel insulted," he said with a little smirk.

"But you don't." She slipped off her sandals, then unfastened her pants and slid them down her hips. A moment later, she stood before him in nothing but her black lace G-string. "Maybe you're a little freaked out that I look so much like Kathryn now."

"Honey, in those panties, you look nothing like your sister." He crossed the room and placed his hands on her waist, then pulled her to him.

"I don't?"

"It doesn't matter how your hair is cut or how much makeup you wear. What makes you Jenna is inside, and a few outward changes don't alter who you are one bit."

Her insides warmed up.

"Ever done it in a dressing room?"

He flashed a devilish smile. "Depends on what you mean by 'it.'"

"This could be your chance. One last time, before I take over Kathryn's life?"

He dipped his head down and covered her mouth with his. Jenna pulled out his shirttail and slid her hands up the hot flesh of his back as he thrust his tongue into her mouth, responding to her with a hunger she hadn't expected. Smooth, always-in-control Travis, she suspected, loved to lose control with her.

She pulled back and nipped at his lip with her teeth, then traced his lips with the tip of her tongue. His erection strained against her lower belly, and Jenna wondered how much time they'd have before Allegra came tapping on the door.

"All these mirrors could be fun," she whispered.

Travis pulled her over to the bench, and she unfastened his pants and took him out. He was hot and ready in her palm, and Jenna felt the urge to take him into her mouth, let him watch in the mirrors as she did it. She pulled him down onto the bench and then knelt between his legs.

When he tried to pull her up, she stayed her ground and dipped her head down, ran her tongue along the length of his erection. He let his head fall back to rest on the mirrored wall and gasped as Jenna took him into her mouth.

She licked and teased and worked him toward the edge, savoring the intimate power she had over his body, enjoying the pulsing heat of him in her mouth. Gently, she dragged her teeth along his rigid length, thrilling at his shudder of pleasure.

She continued to pleasure him with her mouth until his breath was fast and shallow, but just as he was about to reach climax, he stilled her with his hand.

"I want to be inside you," he whispered.

Standing up, she slid her panties down and kicked them aside, then crawled on his lap as he withdrew a condom from his wallet and slipped it on. Without wasting another second, she mounted him and forced his erection as far inside her as it would go. And she began to rock her hips.

"We shouldn't be doing this," he managed to say between gasps.

She stilled her hips and kissed him on the mouth, then trailed her lips to his ear, where she nipped at his earlobe. "You want to stop?"

"Hell no."

"Because I can," she said as she tightened her inner muscles around him.

He grasped her hips and began thrusting into her, fast and hard. Jenna bit her lip to keep her moans silent. She rested her weight on her hands against the mirrored wall, then let her gaze wander to one of the angled mirrors that provided a view of their lovemaking. Watching it was just as hot as experiencing it.

Travis took her breast into his mouth and teased her nipple with his tongue, then made his way to the other one. "You should watch," she whispered.

He stopped and looked at her, his eyes glazed over with arousal, then looked at the mirror she nodded toward. Jenna began to move on him again, rocking her hips in a seductive show, giving him his own impromptu home movie.

But she felt herself coming closer to the edge, felt the tension building inside, and slow and seductive would no longer cut it. She increased the pace again, and in a few moments waves of pleasure washed through her, blinding and unstoppable. Her muscles contracted again and again, and she went limp against Travis just as he came, too.

He muffled their release with a long, deep kiss as he thrust into her one final time, their bodies tensing and then relaxing together.

After a moment, Jenna sat back and looked at him, curious if she would see regret in his gaze. Instead, when he opened his eyes, she saw an emotion she couldn't name. Maybe just desire. Or something more.

"Guess I should try on those clothes."

"Or we could just lock ourselves in here for the rest of the day."

"I think Allegra might call the police."

"Maybe you're right." He kissed her again, and Jenna removed herself from his lap and went in search of her panties and bra.

A knock on the door sounded just as Travis was buckling his belt. "Excuse me? Do you need any help in there?"

"No thanks, just trying to make up our minds," Jenna called out.

"Do you need any other sizes?"

"Um, yes," she improvised, "Maybe a larger size of the flower-print sundress."

"I'll be right back with it," Allegra called through the door.

Jenna smiled at Travis as she tugged a dress off its hanger. By the time the saleswoman was back at the door, Jenna was looking at her sister's image in the mirror again. She opened the door and took the dress.

"That looks lovely on you."

"Thanks, but I'm not sure if I like it." She closed the door again quickly, before Allegra could get a look at their flushed appearances and figure out what they'd really been doing.

Jenna turned back to Travis. "What do you think?"

"It looks like something Kathryn would wear."

She tried on three more outfits, and they picked out the dress and pants and sweater set that fit best, then hurried out of the dressing room with her wearing the summer dress they'd agreed she would meet the Roths in at the family's Independence Day party. It was likely she and Kathryn still wore the exact same size and she'd be able to wear her sister's wardrobe, but Travis wanted her to have a few backup outfits in case Kathryn's clothes didn't fit her perfectly.

After he'd paid a ridiculous amount of money for the two outfits—all the while enduring Allegra's suspicious gaze—they made their way back out into the bright afternoon and looked up and down the street for a restaurant.

"I spotted a place that looked like it had good sandwiches when I was using the phone earlier."

"We're there."

She followed him a block down to a trendy little bistro that had outdoor tables on the sidewalk. They sat down outside, and a waiter quickly brought menus and took their drinks order.

Jenna opened her menu, saw a club sandwich and decided without looking any further that that's what she wanted. She turned her attention to Travis, who closed his menu and looked back at her.

He smiled sheepishly. "We can't let that happen again."

"But you were sort of hoping it would happen, or you wouldn't have followed me into the dressing room."

The waiter set down their drinks and hovered beside the table, waiting for them to order. When they'd placed their orders, he left again, and Jenna pinned Travis with an expectant gaze.

"I'll admit, I was hoping we'd have one more chance to be together before we arrive in Carmel."

"Because once we're there, no more fun, right?"

"Right."

A breeze brushed Jenna's back and neck, reminding her again that her hair had been chopped off. One hand wandered self-consciously up to her bare neck, and she forced it back to her lap.

"So, did the relaxation-weekend plan work for you?" she asked, before taking a sip of her soft drink.

Travis stretched out in his chair and smiled. "I'm feeling more relaxed than I have in months."

"I told you it would work. What about going back to the real world—lots of stress waiting there for you?"

A mysterious look crossed his face. "Maybe I've been inspired to do things a bit differently now."

"How so?"

"I'm not sure. Maybe take a few more risks, spend a little less time trying to please my family."

"Why the change of heart?" Though she had a strong suspicion that one weekend of risk taking had showed him what he'd been missing out on by always playing it safe.

"Let's just say you've given me a different perspective."

"I can't take all the credit. I think things started changing for you with that bar fight."

He shrugged and flashed a sheepish smile. "I felt a little like a caveman defending his territory that night."

Jenna recalled the wild abandon with which they'd made love after the bar fight, and her insides heated. She was going to miss Travis—miss having him in her bed, that is. She had a distinct feeling that once they were back in his everyday world, he'd forget all about her being anything more than the woman he was paying to impersonate Kathryn.

She pushed away a little pang of regret and smiled. "Maybe we should go over the important details for the next two weeks again and make sure I'm not forgetting anything."

"Okay, there's the meeting Wednesday with Paul and Rowena Williams to discuss the land they're considering donating to Kathryn's project. I don't have photos of them, but Blake will be there to introduce you, and I'll try to be there, too, if I can find a good reason…"

Jenna listened, nodding occasionally, as Travis recounted everything they'd gone over in the past two days. Her greatest fear was meeting Blake and having to somehow behave with him as if they were two people deeply in love and about to marry. If she could fool Blake into believing she was Kathryn, she could fool anyone.

But the last thing she wanted was to find herself in a compromising position with her sister's fiancé. Travis had assured her he'd endured listening to countless complaints from Blake in the past weeks about Kathryn's insistence that they not have sex until the wedding, but that wasn't much comfort. She had to somehow get Blake to agree that for the next two weeks, they could have no more physical contact than a chaste kiss on the cheek.

Surely, promises of wild sex to come on the wedding night would be enough to convince him. If there was one thing she knew about her sister, it was that she had pitifully conservative ideas about sex. She probably hadn't even gotten out of the missionary position with Blake, so Jenna had every intention of convincing him that his sex life would get really wild as soon as a ring was on her finger.

Travis continued to drill her with review questions as they ate their lunch and left the restaurant, then began the long drive to Carmel. In the passenger seat, she flipped through her file full of facts about her sister one last time, until it felt as if her head would explode.

Finally, she settled back and watched the scenery of the coastal mountain ranges roll past while distracting Travis from details about Kathryn by asking him about his investment firm. As he explained the workings of it, she was surprised to find herself interested, even fascinated.

When they reached Carmel, they drove through town and then made their way to the outskirts of it along a winding road. When they turned off of the road into a gated driveway, Travis hit a remote control that opened the gate, and they pulled through. After a minute, the house came into view amidst rolling hills. It was a Spanish-style mansion that Jenna was pretty sure she'd seen featured on some California architecture documentary a few years back, and it was even grander than she'd expected.

She glanced over at Travis, who was unfazed by the sight of such an ostentatious home—a mansion he took for granted as just a house where people lived—and she knew in that moment that their fling was truly over. They were in his world now, and she absolutely, positively did not belong.

8

TRAVIS GLANCED at the clock on the dash as he pulled into the driveway of the Roth family estate. They were right on time to slip into the Fourth of July picnic without being noticed. Cars crowded the circular driveway, and a valet dressed in a white coat and white shorts lazed against the short stone wall that lined sections of the garden.

"If anyone asks, I've picked you up from the airport. You just got back into town and couldn't reach anyone else for a ride."

Jenna stared at the house. "You didn't tell me your family lives in one of California's great landmark homes."

"You didn't ask," he joked, but her expression made it clear she wasn't in the mood for joking.

"I don't think I can do this."

Travis did a double take at the uncertainty in her voice. He'd quickly come to take it for granted that Jenna was certain about everything, that she had the sort of unshakable confidence that made her comfortable in any situation.

"If most everyone can do it, you can. You've

seen pictures of anyone you'll need to recognize, you've gone over all the facts you need to know— you'll be fine."

"But—"

"I'll be staying close by and watching in case you get into any sticky situations. Just use our signal."

"I'm supposed to make eye contact with you and scratch my nose?"

"Right."

"What if I can't get your attention?"

"I don't think you'll have to worry about that." The bigger worry was if he'd ever be able to take his eyes *off* Jenna, whether anyone else would see the hunger in his gaze when he looked at her.

Travis pulled up to the curb and the valet opened the door for Jenna. Once they were both out of the car and the valet was pulling it away, Travis showed her the way through the house, taking advantage of the fact that everyone was outside to acquaint her with what her sister already knew about the house.

Once they'd finished the quick tour, Travis led the way to the rear lawn where the party was in full swing. His parents had been throwing this Fourth of July celebration every year for as long as he could remember, and some things about it never changed. There was always a quartet playing big band tunes, there was always an array of striped tents throughout the yard shading guests from the harsh sun and there was always his mother drinking a little too much champagne.

"Don't forget," he whispered as they stepped out onto the rear veranda, "my mother could be a little tipsy. Take whatever she says in stride."

Jenna nodded as she surveyed the crowd. "I'm mainly worried about your brother. What if he tries to cram his tongue down my throat the moment he sees me?"

"I've never seen your sister indulge in a public display of affection, so this is the best possible place for you to meet Blake. Just do what we rehearsed."

She took a deep breath and exhaled. "Right."

"We'd better start mingling."

He figured the best bet was to introduce Jenna to Blake right away and get the worst over with, so he scanned the crowd until he spotted his brother chatting up an old business associate.

They wandered across the lawn, and Blake cut off his conversation as soon as he spotted Jenna.

"There's my lovely fiancée!" He embraced his faux fiancée with the enthusiasm of a guy who had no clue he was hugging the wrong woman, then made an attempt to kiss her. Jenna offered up her cheek, then gave him a chaste peck on the cheek, as well.

Blake smiled at her playfully, undaunted by the lack of a mouth kiss. Travis's theory that Kathryn didn't like public affection had been solid, thank God.

"How was the flight home?" Blake asked.

Jenna flashed a charming smile. "Uneventful. I spent the whole time thinking about seeing you again."

Yep, she had her sister pegged. She knew her speech patterns and mannerisms even better than Travis had hoped. He relaxed by another degree and turned his attention to the business associate Blake had been talking to, letting the fake lovebirds have a little time together.

After a few minutes, Blake led Jenna off to mingle, and Travis found himself almost completely relaxed. Until he spotted his mother headed straight for them, half-empty champagne glass in hand.

Even under the influence of alcohol, Georgina Roth had a keen radar for bullshit. She was Jenna's biggest test, especially considering how she was always looking for something wrong with Kathryn anyway. Travis excused himself from his business associate and made his way toward Blake and Jenna, arriving just as their mother did.

"Kathryn, it's so good to see you could make it back in time for the party," Georgina said in a tone that made it clear she wasn't all that happy to see her future daughter-in-law.

"Hello, Mrs. Roth."

"Do tell me all about your stay at the spa. You're looking quite relaxed, I must say."

Jenna cast a glance at Travis, and he quickly

looked down at his shoes. "It *was* very relaxing," she said.

"I trust you feel all rested up for the wedding festivities."

"Absolutely."

"Because you know, once you're married, you won't be able to flit away for little solo retreats."

"*Mom.*" Blake intervened. "Kathryn can do whatever she pleases when we're married."

Georgina cast him a withering glance. "Careful what you say now, son."

Jenna seemed at a loss for words, but then she smiled sweetly and gave Blake's arm a pat. "I can't imagine wanting to leave my husband's side. This vacation was only to help me look my best for Blake at the wedding."

"You already looked perfect," Blake said.

Their mother downed the remainder of her champagne and daintily placed the glass on a nearby table. When she turned back to them, Travis could tell by the smug look in her eyes she wasn't finished with Kathryn.

"I do hope you've rethought that whole women's shelter idea. I simply don't see how you'll have the time or the know-how to oversee it."

"I've quit my job at the, um, gallery," Jenna said, her cheeks coloring at her stumble. "And I'll learn as I go."

Georgina couldn't have had any real objection to the women's shelter, but she liked to put up a good front. It wasn't like his mother to be so uncharitable, and Travis suspected her reservations stemmed more from a fear of Blake and Kathryn flaking out on the project once it lost its luster, thereby tarnishing the precious Roth name.

One good thing about their mother was that, unlike their father, Georgina knew the capabilities of her sons.

"Perhaps all your pageant training will help you relate better to the women at the shelters," his mother said in her most vitriolic tone.

Jenna blinked. Travis realized he hadn't quite done an adequate job of preparing her for how condescending his mother could be to Kathryn. It was a testament to Kathryn's love for Blake that she put up with such crap.

And then Jenna flashed a sly smile that was all vixen, not her sister's smile at all. Travis steeled himself for impending disaster. "Absolutely. I can show them how to tape their breasts together for maximum cleavage during job interviews."

It wasn't like Kathryn to make sarcastic jokes, but Blake apparently didn't notice. He laughed, then Jenna joined in, and Travis forced himself to laugh, too. Their mother looked at the three of them as if they'd grown horns.

"That's exactly the sort of attitude that makes it clear to me this project will be a disaster with you running it." She snatched a new glass of champagne from a passing waiter and turned on her heel, then marched off.

Jenna sobered when she realized the damage

she'd done slipping out of character. "Sorry," she said, "I shouldn't have taunted your mother like that."

"She was asking for it. I'm glad to see you finally put her in her place like I've told you to do," Blake said.

Travis tried to pass Jenna a silent look that said all was okay, but before she could see him, he was accosted by Natalie Wentworth, whose timing could not have been worse.

He'd dated Natalie on and off over the years, theirs being a relationship based more on the convenience of sex without commitment than anything else. She was driven to make it to the top of her law firm unhindered by marriage and family obligations, and she had a great set of legs.

He'd been avoiding her recently, though, growing tired of the lack of emotional involvement, but she slipped her arm around his waist and kissed him as if they were still lovers.

When he'd finally untangled himself from her, he caught Jenna's look of confusion.

"Um, Natalie, you remember Blake and his fiancée Kathryn, right?"

"Of course. I'm sure you two won't mind if I steal Travis away for a short while."

Blake flashed his most charming smile. "Of course not. He's just being a third wheel anyway."

Jenna forced a smile, but for all her talk of no-strings-attached sex for the weekend, Travis had the distinct feeling there were strings. Hell, he knew there were, because he felt them tugging him toward her every minute of the day.

IF THIS PARTY DIDN'T END SOON, Jenna feared she'd succumb to the urge to drown herself in the Roth's gigantic Italianate water fountain. She'd slipped away from Blake with the excuse that she wanted to chat with a friend, and then she'd managed to avoid conversation with anyone for a good while by wandering around, snacking on finger foods and trying to look as if she were searching for someone.

Ever since Travis had been lured away by the Nicole Kidman look-alike, Jenna had been fighting a battle inside herself not to care that he was involved with another woman. She had absolutely no reason to care, after all. She wasn't interested in him in anything more than a sexual way, and she certainly wasn't foolish enough to think their weekend of sex was going to blossom into a real love affair.

Hell, she didn't even want a real love affair.... Did she? Her philosophy about men had always been to take advantage of opportunities as they came along, but never to go looking for love. If it found her, then it was meant to be.

And for her entire adult life, that philosophy had worked out just fine. She'd never encountered a man like Travis before, though, a man who lingered in her thoughts constantly, whose body fit with hers as if it had been made to please her—

and a man who was so altogether wrong for her
that she'd be a fool to let her heart get involved.

As Jenna made her way around the lawn and
garden, admiring the Roth family's stunning estate, she willed herself not to look for Travis. Instead, she spotted Blake wandering nearby, clearly
looking for his fiancée, and she ducked behind
the ice sculpture.

This charade was even worse than she'd feared
it would be. Every time Blake came near, she felt
like a sleaze and a fraud, and she wanted to scream
that she wasn't at all who he thought she was.

"Kathryn! It's so lovely to see you."

Jenna turned to find a woman standing beside
her, a woman she had the distinct feeling she was
supposed to recognize. She plastered on a smile
and said, "Isn't this a beautiful party?"

"Oh, absolutely. The Roths always hold such
fabulous shindigs."

Shindigs? Did people really talk that way?

"So how have you been?" Jenna asked, figuring
it was about as benign a question as there was.

"You *know* I've been absolutely horrid ever
since that awful incident with Ryan."

Jenna produced what she hoped was a vague
look of sympathy and nodded.

Her Chanel-clad companion frowned. "Is
something wrong, Kathryn? You seem distracted."

"I'm sorry. You actually caught me on my way
to the ladies' room."

"By all means, don't let me hold you up. I just

have one quick question—do you think I should tell him the truth?"

Uh-oh. "Um, Ryan, you mean?"

"Of course. Who else?"

The truth was rarely a bad thing, right? Could she go wrong advising honesty?

"Yes, I...definitely think you should."

The woman's eyes widened. "Are you *sure?*"

"Well..." Jenna glanced around, wishing Travis would magically appear and keep her from having to answer.

"No, you're right. I will tell him. Right now. The sooner, the better."

Jenna wasn't sure if the decision required a smile or a solemn nod. The woman seemed nervous, so she opted for a nod and excused herself. On her way to the bathroom, Blake spotted her and made a beeline in her direction. Jenna considered dodging and running, but she figured she'd have to face her sister's fiancé again sooner or later, so she stopped and produced a smile.

"Darling, I've been looking all over for you." Blake slid his arm around her waist and pulled her close. "I don't want to let you out of my sight for another minute."

Jenna offered her cheek when he leaned in for a kiss, and he pulled back and eyed her as if she'd just suggested they go shopping at a discount store. "What's with the cheek thing. Is something the matter?"

"There are just so many people here."

"Forget about them. We're nearly newlyweds. They expect us not to be able to keep our hands off of each other."

Okay, this was her opportunity. "Blakey," she said, using the term of endearment Travis had mentioned was her sister's favorite, "Speaking of keeping our hands off of each other..."

"Tell me you've come to your senses," he said, lowering his voice.

"This period of waiting is just as hard for me as it is for you, but I was thinking during my visit to the spa, we could make our honeymoon night even more exciting..."

He smiled, slid his hand down to her hip, and Jenna resisted the urge to slap it away.

"Oh yeah?"

"If we don't have any sort of physical contact for the next two weeks."

Blake's expression went from flirtatious to horrified. He turned to face her and took her hands in his. "Are you crazy?"

It did sound pretty crazy when spoken out loud. Okay, so she could improvise. "I read a book, a sort of sex manual, at the spa, in preparation," she said, lowering her voice to a seductive purr. "And I learned quite a bit, including the effects of a period of complete physical abstinence on the following sexual experience."

Blake's frown disappeared. "A sex manual, hmm? What else did you learn from it?"

"Oh, lots of things, lots of naughty, naughty

things that I cannot wait to try out with you. On our wedding night."

"Like what?" he whispered, smiling and nodding at a middle-aged couple passing by.

"I learned things too scandalous to say out loud in a public place, but once I have you alone in our honeymoon suite, you'll never want to leave."

Blake's eyes dilated, and his breathing grew shallow. "Can't we at least do a little premarital kissing?"

"Not for the effect to be complete." She paused and licked her lips slowly. "Trust me, you won't regret practicing some restraint. It's only two short weeks."

"Maybe I should read that book, too. In preparation."

Oops. Jenna frowned, trying to remember if she'd ever actually read such a book. She had been exposed to plenty of sex manuals in her freelance research, but she had no idea if any of them prescribed strict periods of abstinence.

"I might have left it at the spa by accident. But I'll double-check. Maybe I can find a copy for you at a local bookstore."

Blake tilted his head to the side and offered her a puppy-dog frown. "I don't know if I can survive all that waiting."

"It's not even two weeks—really just a week and five days."

"Can't I get one last little kiss on the mouth to hold me over?"

"No cheating." She flashed her most seductive smile. "I promise, I'll make it worth the wait." She leaned in and gave Blake a brief peck on the cheek, then withdrew her hands from his.

He expelled a ragged sigh but made no further protest.

"I need to make a trip to the little girls' room," Jenna said, spouting the cutesy language her sister favored.

Blake smiled. "Don't be gone long. If I can't touch you, I at least want to be able to see you."

Jenna wiggled her fingers at him and hurried off toward the main house. Rest room signs designated the pool house as the place for guests to go, but she needed to get as far away from the crowd as possible.

Once inside, she wandered down the hallway trying to remember where she'd seen the bathroom earlier, but the sound of Travis's voice coming from a nearby room caught her attention.

"Yes, that sounds like the way to go. First thing, as soon as the market opens tomorrow," he was saying as Jenna followed the sound to the open door of a study.

Travis sat at a cherry executive desk talking on the phone. Relieved to see the one person who didn't think she was Kathryn, Jenna hovered in the doorway, not wanting to interrupt but unable to leave. When he hung up the phone, Travis swiveled around in the black leather office chair and spotted her.

"Sorry, I didn't mean to interrupt your work," she said. "No day off on the Fourth of July?"

"Just one phone call."

"Mind if I hide out in here for a few minutes?" she asked, forcing herself not to inquire about the whereabouts of his female friend.

Travis stood up and came to the door, where he peered out and down the hallway. "Did anyone see you come in here?"

"No."

"We have to be careful," he said, closing the door to the study.

Jenna felt as if her body temperature rose several degrees in such close proximity to Travis, alone. He turned to face her, and she knew by his expression that he was suffering from a bit of over-heating himself.

"I should leave," she said half-heartedly.

"Yes."

"But you don't want me to."

Travis turned the lock on the doorknob, then crossed the room and closed the shades.

Jenna lowered her voice to a whisper as she walked to the desk. "Blake cornered me, but I think I've got him under control."

"So he knows that you don't want any physical contact before the wedding?"

"He thinks I got the idea from a sex manual."

Travis smiled. "Good thinking. I'm sorry I haven't been able to stick close to you like I promised."

"It's okay, you have other obligations."

"Please don't get the wrong idea about Natalie. She and I used to be involved, but we haven't been together in months."

"It's none of my business, but you looked pretty obviously together an hour ago," Jenna said, hating the tone of her voice.

"I made it clear to her that I no longer want to be anything more than friends. She understands where I'm coming from, and she's okay with it."

"I hope you didn't do that on my account."

"I did it because I wanted to." He came to her side and leaned against the desk, letting his gaze travel down the length of her and back up.

His nearness made her forget about everything but the heat between them, and Jenna knew he felt it, too. Otherwise, he wouldn't have been coming so close to violating his own hands-off rules.

"Too bad I'm off limits for you, too," she said, her voice sounding more breathless than she'd intended.

"I didn't realize how hard this would be."

Jenna imagined inching herself closer, demanding one last kiss, but she knew one kiss would never be enough. If she kissed him, she'd have to touch him, and if she touched him, she'd have to make love to him, too.

"Me, either," she whispered.

"I should get back out to the party. I've been away too long."

"I do have one question first. Do you know anything about a man named Ryan and his blond significant other?"

He frowned. "Ryan Case and his fiancée, Madeline. I forgot to give you a photo of them."

"I may have caused a bit of trouble. She asked me some advice about 'telling Ryan the truth,' and I told her she definitely should. Any idea what she was talking about?"

Travis winced. "I'm afraid so. I believe she plans on admitting to him that she's a lesbian."

"Oh. She made some comment about an incident with him recently."

"He caught her with another woman, but she somehow managed to explain it away."

"Like, 'Oh my, I just accidentally fell on this naked woman lying on my bed'?"

Travis smiled. "Something like that."

"Maybe you should talk to her, at least keep her from causing a scene here at your parents' party."

Travis stood up from the edge of the desk and ran one hand through his hair. "Good idea," he said, but he lingered at her side.

"If you stay here, I'm going to kiss you."

His gaze lingered on her, and she could almost see the battle raging inside him. Just when she thought he was going to leave, he closed the distance between them and slipped one hand around her waist. With the other, he cupped the back of her head.

When his gaze locked on her mouth, she knew he'd kiss her, and it was exactly what she'd been aching for him to do.

9

TRAVIS COVERED Jenna's mouth with his, then lingered there. She snaked her arms around his neck and savored the taste and feel of him, slipped her tongue inside his mouth and reminded herself of why she loved kissing him so much.

A moment later, he pulled back. "Damn it."

"Yeah. Damn it."

"We can't be alone anymore together, if this is what's going to happen."

"Right," she said, resisting the urge to rip his shirt open and lick his chest.

"I'm sorry I let my control slip. I know that only makes this harder." He stepped back, and Jenna let her arms fall to her sides.

Travis went to the door and opened it, looked out into the hallway, then turned and nodded for her to go.

Out of nowhere, her desire turned into a sense of violation. Maybe Travis wasn't just concerned about ruining their charade, or getting caught having an affair with his brother's "fiancée." Maybe it was just her. Maybe she'd been right all along that he might have considered her worthy of a few nights in the sack, but that once they were in his world, he couldn't lower himself to her level.

Okay, she could suck it up. She wasn't going to let some arrogant, spoiled rich guy get under her skin. She left the office without giving him a second glance, but she'd only made it as far as the back door when Blake found her again.

"Hey sweetheart, I thought you might have fallen in."

Jenna smiled at his lame joke as if he were brilliant. "I just needed a little quiet. I guess all the noise and heat are getting to me."

"What do you say we skip the fireworks display and have a little intimate fireworks show of our own?"

Ugh, this guy was a broken record, *and* he couldn't take no for an answer.

"I'm not sure intimate is a good idea if we want to keep our pact," she said in her best coy female imitation.

"Hmm, I guess you're not going to change your mind." He frowned. "How about dinner instead? If we're in a restaurant, we'll be forced to behave ourselves, right?"

Jenna groaned inwardly. She'd have to be alone for an evening with Blake sooner or later, so she supposed it made sense to get it over with as soon as possible.

"Sure, you name the place, and I'll meet you there, okay?"

"But what about slipping out of here early with me? You're my excuse to leave."

"Just tell anyone who asks that you need to freshen up for our big date."

He smiled and tugged her close. "Okay then, we'll behave, and I'll see you, say, around seven at Sylvio's?"

Sure, she'd just have to figure out where the heck Sylvio's was. No problem. "It's a plan."

Jenna gave him a quick peck on the cheek and tried to slip out of his grasp, but he held on. "It's odd, but I feel like something is different about you today."

Jenna shrugged. "It's amazing what a little relaxation can do for a girl."

He clearly wasn't convinced that she was simply more relaxed, but he shrugged. "Maybe. I can't put my finger on what seems different."

Her heart pounded in her ears, but he mercifully let her go. She could feel his gaze following her as she went out onto the back lawn again. She wandered around trying to look occupied with a glass of seltzer water, until she got the distinct feeling she was being watched.

Glancing around, her gaze finally settled on a woman sitting alone at a nearby table. She wore sunglasses and what Jenna would have bet money was a wig, and something about her looked oddly familiar. She studied the woman for a moment as she hailed a waiter for another drink, but she had no idea where she might have seen her before.

Jenna did a mental shrug and decided she was letting the stress get to her.

Then she spotted Travis outside again. Jenna made her way over to him and tried to act as if he wasn't someone she'd had sex with in a dressing room earlier that day.

"I've got a date with Blake for tonight."

He winced. "I guess that was inevitable. Maybe I can load him down with work this week to keep him away from you as much as possible."

"I think I can handle him for tonight. We're supposed to meet at a place called Sylvio's."

"I can give you directions, but first we'll need to slip out of here so I can show you the way to Kathryn's place."

"How about you make your excuses and I'll meet you out front in another ten minutes?"

"It could be harder leaving together than it was showing up. Why don't I call you a cab to Kathryn's place, and then I'll leave at the same time and follow you there?"

Jenna nodded, and they parted ways. She wandered around the party a bit more, aware of the sensation of someone watching her. She scanned the crowd and didn't see anyone. Probably it was Travis keeping tabs on her whereabouts.

But then she spotted Travis with his back to her as he talked to his father. Jenna surveyed the crowd again, and her gaze landed on the woman in the wig and sunglasses. She seemed to be staring straight at Jenna, her expression neutral. Jenna watched her for a few moments, and the woman looked away.

Maybe the woman recognized her from somewhere, or maybe she could tell she was a fraud. Maybe she knew Kathryn was still at the spa... No, impossible.

If Blake couldn't tell his own fiancée from an imposter, then it wasn't likely anyone else could, either. Kathryn had sworn to Travis that no one else knew about her not coming back from the spa, and Jenna couldn't imagine her sister having spilled the secret to anyone that she'd had a botched plastic surgery.

Jenna managed to slip out of the party without any questions, saying an awkward goodbye to Mr. and Mrs. Roth without enduring any more abuse from the latter.

Fifteen minutes later her cab was pulling into the driveway of an oceanside postmodern concoction of windows and redwood that Jenna imagined her sister planned to transform into a showplace that would lure the likes of *Architectural Digest* to do a feature. It wasn't exactly Jenna's taste, but it was impressive. Kathryn Calvert had certainly moved up in the world.

She paid the driver and wandered up to the front entrance, noting the equally stark-looking landscape design Blake had probably paid some landscape architect a horrifying sum to plant. Before she reached the door, Travis pulled into the drive, and she couldn't help but catch her breath at the sight of him, a vision of male perfection, driving the sleek little Mercedes.

When he reached the top of the steps, he said, "Nice view, huh?"

Jenna had been so caught up marveling at the house and landscaping that she'd failed to look out beyond the surrounding trees to the ocean. She followed the sound of crashing waves to see that her sister's house had a stunning view of the Pacific from every front window. The view alone probably cost as much as most houses.

"Blake bought this place?" she asked.

He nodded. "They didn't want to start out in something that had belonged to either of them when they were single. Kathryn has been living here for a few months, getting it all set up."

"How about a grand tour then?"

Travis withdrew a key from his pocket and handed it to her. "You wouldn't believe what I had to go through to get this. Blake spent an entire day ranting about having lost his keys while I made a copy."

She opened the door and went inside with Travis following. "I guess you shouldn't stay long."

"I'll just give you a quick tour and get out of here before someone spots my car."

He led the way through the house, giving explanations of whatever he knew about. Jenna recognized her sister in almost every detail. It felt weird walking around Kathryn's house without her there, as if she were trespassing. By the time

Travis had finished the tour, Jenna had the vague feeling of having been reacquainted with Kathryn by snooping—even if it was approved snooping.

"Thanks for showing me around," she said.

"I have to admit, it was just an excuse to get you alone again."

"You love temptation," she said, looking out the window at a ship passing far in the distance.

"I can think of worse kinds of torture." He leaned against the window ledge, smiling a weary smile.

"You look tired."

"I didn't get much sleep last night."

"Oh, right." She smiled at the memory of their lovemaking, which had lasted well into the early morning hours. "I know how you feel—being my sister is exhausting."

"Let's hope Kathryn shows up sooner rather than later. Next time she calls I'll make sure she understands what a hard time you're having putting off Blake. That ought to convince her to come home."

Jenna frowned at the thought of Kathryn not showing up until the last minute. The prospect was just too much to dwell on. "I guess you'd better go, huh?"

Travis was watching her mouth, as if transfixed. "That kiss at my parents' house? I don't regret it."

"But it can't happen again."

"I guess not."

"You don't sound very convinced."

"I don't seem to have much self-control when you're around."

Jenna shrugged. "Sometimes a little indulgence is just what you need."

"But not right now."

"No. So I promise I'll try not to tempt you, okay?" She couldn't help but smile at the idea of turning off the chemistry between them. It was impossible.

"Good luck with the dinner tonight. Call me when you get home and let me know how it went."

"You think I'll survive?" she asked, suddenly realizing what a miserable evening she had to look forward to, nothing like the previous few nights of bliss she'd spent with Travis.

"I think you'll do great. And if something goes wrong, it's not the end of the world."

Jenna quirked an eyebrow. "That's a pretty cavalier attitude you've suddenly developed."

"Another one of your effects on me."

He should have left then, but he lingered by her side at the window, watching her through half-lidded eyes.

What she would have given to drag him over to the sofa and make love to him again, but it would be a huge mistake now. And so would kissing him. Yep, big mistake.

Big, big mistake.

Travis finally broke their strange standoff, pushing himself away from the window. He found his keys in his pocket and headed for the door, and a minute later Jenna was watching through the window as he drove away.

She turned around to face the house and sighed into the silence. This was her sister's home, a place she would have been completely unwelcome a week ago, a place she wouldn't even have imagined setting foot in last week.

Jenna wandered through each room again, spotting photos of Kathryn and Blake looking blissfully happy, Kathryn and Blake looking amused, Kathryn and Blake posing for stylish black-and-white engagement photos. There were also a few photos of each set of parents, a few shots here and there of people Jenna recognized as Kathryn's friends.

The entire house was painstakingly organized, obsessively neat, hardly marred by a speck of dust. In the kitchen, she opened the cabinets to confirm her suspicion that Kathryn had organized the dry and canned goods alphabetically and by category.

Typical. In their younger years when they'd been forced to share a room, Kathryn's side had always been perfectly kept, while Jenna's side was always a little messy, a little cluttered—and always a point of contention between the two.

Jenna laughed at a long-forgotten memory of a fight they'd had some time in their preteen years over the state of Jenna's side of the room that had resulted in each of them scalping the other's favorite Barbie doll.

She had the sudden and foreign urge to see Kathryn at that moment, to reminisce with her about old times, to just hang out like normal sisters would. It must have been all the stress of the afternoon getting to her. Clearly, she needed a stiff drink and a good night's sleep, and she'd wake up tomorrow free of any misguided sisterly feelings.

A clock on the wall reminded her that she had less than an hour to get ready for her intimate evening with her sister's fiancé. Jenna decided that was an even better excuse for a stiff drink, but she needed a clear head for the evening's acting session. If she could survive tonight, she told herself as she climbed the stairs to Kathryn's bedroom, she could survive the next two weeks no problem.

Yep, right. No problem.

JENNA SAT IN KATHRYN'S CAR in the parking lot of Roth Investments, strumming her fingers on the steering wheel and trying not to hyperventilate.

It was only her fifth day impersonating Kathryn, and already she was ready to forget the money and run for the hills. She'd barely survived the Fourth of July dinner with Blake, and she'd narrowly avoided disaster at a family dinner yesterday night when Blake's parents started asking her questions about the women and children's shelter project—questions she'd been forced to make up answers to.

Jenna had miraculously managed to dodge Blake for most of the week, thanks in part to Travis inventing extra tasks to keep his brother busy at work, and when she wasn't being Kathryn, she'd found plenty of time to start reconstructing her research and her outline of the pageant-industry article. Travis had loaned her a laptop to work on, but she hadn't felt as much zeal for the project as she'd expected. Her mind was frequently occupied with other thoughts.

Thoughts of one particularly delicious guy in a suit whom she'd also not seen much of this week. Mentally she understood their need to avoid each other, but physically, his absence was more painful than she'd expected. The nights since last weekend had been especially long.

But even in her most passionate love affairs, she'd always been able to keep her mind on the job when it was necessary. It drove Jenna mad to feel so scatterbrained, to find herself staring out the window and daydreaming of Travis whenever she should have been working. She was behaving more like a lovesick schoolgirl than a grown woman, and she'd resolved to put him out of her mind for good.

That should have been no problem, except that she'd be seeing him again in a matter of minutes, and her every nerve ending was on alert. He'd expressed an interest in the women and children's shelter project in order to be present for Jenna and Blake's meeting with Paul and Rowena Williams, the couple with the land to donate.

Jenna glanced at her watch, cursed herself for arriving so early and decided to go in. She entered the gleaming glass office building and found out from the receptionist where the meeting would be held, then followed the directions given to a large, meticulously clean meeting room, complete with a huge conference table and chairs for everyone.

She selected a chair and sat down with her folder of notes, prepared to study the information Travis had given her about Kathryn's charity project in the twenty minutes before the meeting was to begin. But then the sound of the door opening caught her attention, and she looked up to see Travis fill the doorway.

"Hey," was the wittiest thing she could think to say as her body responded to him with all the heat of a blazing inferno. She resisted the urge to fan herself.

"Hey, yourself." He smiled and closed the door, then took a seat next to her.

"How did you know I was here?"

"I asked the receptionist to call me when you arrived."

"Shouldn't we be worried about someone walking in and wondering why we're here alone?" Jenna asked, glancing at the door.

"We're just the first two people to arrive for the meeting. I was hoping you'd get here early."

"Because?"

"Because this has been a long week."

Jenna suppressed a smile. So, he'd felt the same agony she had. The thought was inexplicably satisfying. "Which is exactly why we shouldn't be here alone."

He flashed her a devilish look. "Afraid you can't control yourself around me?"

She wet her lips and leaned forward, placing a hand on his thigh under the table. "Is it *my* self-control we really have to worry about?"

It was a cruel, cruel trick, but she couldn't help toying with him just a little to see if she could make his cool, polished facade disappear.

He shifted in his seat. "Point taken." Jenna removed her hand from his thigh, and he seemed to relax by a degree. "I actually wanted to tell you I heard back from the private investigator today."

"Oh?"

"He hasn't found anything suspicious, other than what has gone on between us."

"I told you there was no reason to worry about us being followed, but what about this guy? Would he tell anyone that you're messing around with your brother's woman?"

"He knows you're not Kathryn. It was the only way to make sure he could do his job."

Jenna nodded, flattered that he'd risk ruining his and Kathryn's scheme for her safety. Again she found herself savoring the feeling of someone looking out for her. It was nice to feel as if she wasn't alone, as if it wasn't just her against the world, even if her guardian angel was only a temporary one.

She was also aware now of the strange sensation of being near Travis when he was not available to her. She couldn't touch him, couldn't confess secrets to him, couldn't share private smiles with him once anyone else was present. She hadn't realized how badly she'd want to continue where they'd left off Monday or how frustrated she'd feel now that they could be no more than casual acquaintances.

This kind of turmoil was *so* not what she'd had in mind when she'd made her deal with Travis.

The sound of the turning doorknob caught their attention, and Jenna looked up to see Blake enter the room.

"Hey, am I actually early for the first time in my life?" Blake said as he went to Jenna and placed a kiss on her forehead.

"It appears so," Travis said.

Jenna quelled her disappointment that she'd lost her chance to be alone with Travis, reminding herself that the situation could only have led to more trouble. It was a good thing Blake had showed up. Really, it was.

Blake gave Travis a curious look. "There's been something strange about you this week. You aren't your usual uptight self. What gives?"

Jenna watched the battle of emotions in Travis's eyes. She couldn't have said exactly what he was feeling, but he was definitely conflicted.

"I don't know what you're talking about."

"You haven't given me a single stern lecture this week, and you keep bebopping around the office like a kid on the day before summer break."

"I haven't been *bebopping*."

Jenna bit her lip to keep from laughing.

"And what's with the decision to buy all that stock in Yoshiro Electronics? That's the riskiest move you've ever made."

Travis shrugged. "I believe in the company."

"See what I mean? You hardly sound like yourself. You never make a big move like that without spouting a long list of statistics and research."

Jenna felt a self-satisfied smile settle on her lips. She'd had an impact on Travis, and a positive one, by the sounds of it.

"I decided to go with my gut this time," Travis said without offering any further explanation.

"If I didn't know better, I'd say you were getting seriously laid."

"What do you mean 'if you didn't know better'? What do you know about my sex life?"

"I know it has cobwebs growing on it," Blake said as he leaned back in his chair and propped his feet on the table.

Jenna couldn't help it—she laughed out loud—and Blake smiled at her as if they were sharing a favorite joke.

"Believe that if you want," Travis said with a shrug, and Jenna saw in Blake's expression disappointment that he couldn't get a rise out of his brother.

"See what I mean? You're being way too casual. You *are* getting laid, aren't you? Are you and Natalie doing the nasty again?"

Jenna recalled the elegant woman who'd accosted Travis at the Fourth of July party. She looked like the kind of woman he belonged with, and Jenna wondered if Travis had told her the whole story on Natalie.

Not that it was any of her business.

The receptionist who'd directed Jenna to the meeting room earlier stuck her head inside the door, then opened it wide for a middle-aged couple Jenna assumed were the Williamses.

Jenna took a deep breath and willed herself to relax and think Kathryn thoughts. No more fantasizing about Travis, and no more chuckling about his sex life.

This was it, the most important part of her job, making sure Kathryn's charity project got the land it needed. She may not have cared for helping her sister, but she wanted the women and children's shelter to be a success.

And if she had her way, it would be.

10

IF TRAVIS HAD TO ENDURE one more minute of pretending Jenna was his brother's fiancée, he was going to hit something. He stood up from the arm of the sofa and stalked across the room, tension coiled inside him. He felt ready to spring at the nearest object in his path.

His parents had thrown a cocktail party tonight to welcome Jenna's parents to Carmel, and Jenna had survived the ultimate test—convincing her own mother that she was Kathryn. But Travis wasn't entirely sure *he* was going to survive the rest of the evening.

For the past week and a half, they'd managed to avoid any major incidents, and no one had guessed that "Kathryn" was a fraud. Maybe a few people had noticed she wasn't quite behaving like herself, but they had no reason to question the issue.

Jenna even seemed to have relaxed into the role. But Travis, on the other hand, was a mess. He was barely sleeping at night, taking cold showers at odd hours and generally not giving a damn about work. Actually, that last change was pretty refreshing. It felt liberating not to be worried about the countless details of running the business.

He should have been happy with the way the whole scheme had worked out. Not only had Jenna done a good job, she'd been fabulous at convincing the Williamses to donate their land to Kathryn's charity project, and that alone should have been enough to put Travis at ease.

But it wasn't. Because what he really wanted was Jenna, all to himself.

And then there was the whole issue of the real Kathryn, who still hadn't shown up and had been very noncommittal when he'd spoken to her yesterday. In spite of her insistence that she wouldn't miss the wedding, she wouldn't say when she'd be back in town. The swelling, she claimed, was still too noticeable.

"I'd like to propose a toast," Blake was saying for the tenth time—his words slurring so that propose came out "proposh"—"to my lovely Kathryn."

Travis halted at the door, unable to look away from the spectacle. Blake never could handle his liquor.

People standing close by looked at each other, apparently wondering if they really would be forced to toast Kathryn yet again, but then Blake raised his martini glass to the Tiffany lamp next to him and clinked it against the shade.

Jenna managed to look affectionately tolerant standing at Blake's side, but when he reached out and placed one hand on her backside, she slipped away from his grasp. Her gaze sought Travis out, and she gave him a pleading look.

He nodded as discreetly as he could toward the door, and after a moment, he turned and walked out, furious with himself for jumping at another opportunity to be alone with her. He practically ran down the hallway to the foyer and stood there stiff with tension. Was he really about to do something as tawdry as slip into the coat closet with his brother's fake fiancée?

A moment later, Jenna stepped out into the hallway and spotted him. The delicate lavender dress she wore draped her curves in a way that suggested both innocence and raw sexuality. He could see the outline of her breasts and hips, the delicious hint of cleavage at her bodice. He probably never would have noticed Kathryn in the dress, but on Jenna, knowing the vixen the dress concealed…

Yes. Yes, he was.

Jenna cast a glance toward the parlor and then came toward him. Before anyone could spot him, Travis opened the coat-closet door and slipped inside—not a difficult task considering this wasn't the coat-wearing season. Closing the door all but a crack, he found himself surrounded by ladies' shawls and a few sportcoats, the scents of cedar and unidentifiable perfumes and colognes mingling in the air.

He'd just cleared a spot for both of them to stand in when Jenna opened the door and stepped inside, then closed it behind her. Heat flooded his body in that instant, just as darkness closed in around them. After a few moments, he could see Jenna by the light under the door.

"We shouldn't be here," she whispered, taking a step closer and pressing her body against him, pinning him to the wall.

He slid his hands down over her hips and savored the feel of her. "Right. We should go back to the party before someone notices we're both missing."

"I'm going to murder Blake if I have to spend another minute with him."

"He's not your type?" he joked.

"He's like a young, WASP version of Homer Simpson."

Travis warned himself not to feel flattered. After all, he wasn't her type, either. He was just her temporary stress reliever.

He didn't have to worry about a response, because she kissed him then—a long, deep kiss that made him forget for the duration of it that they were in his parents' coat closet. It was only when she pulled away that he remembered.

"What if I go back in and tell everyone I'm not feeling well, then bow out early?" she whispered, breathless.

"We'd be breaking our no-contact rule."

"We already are," she said and slid her hand down, grasping his erection to make her point.

Travis closed his eyes and groaned down low in his throat. The past week and a half hadn't gone at all the way he'd planned, and now he wanted nothing more than to take Jenna home and make love to her all night.

In spite of his better judgment warning him that someone could decide to leave early and open the coat closet at any moment, he cupped her face in his hand and kissed her again, then let his other hand find her rigid nipple through the thin fabric of her dress.

"What the—"

Light flooded the closet, and Travis looked up to see his father standing in the doorway, red-faced and working up to what he knew was going to be an earsplitting bellow if he didn't intervene fast.

"Dad, wait. Let me explain—"

"Both of you, upstairs, now!" Roland Roth nearly growled.

His father turned and stormed up the stairs. Jenna gave Travis a wide-eyed look.

"I'm so sorry," she whispered as she straightened her dress, then slipped out of his grasp and peered into the foyer. "All's clear."

Travis followed her up the stairs, surprised at the lack of fear in his gut. He felt, oddly, almost relieved at his dad's discovery. Maybe even a little victorious in some perverse way, as if he'd finally been found out as a man of his own choosing.

At the top of the stairs, they could see Roland standing in the hallway outside his den. He stood with his arms crossed and an angry glare plastered on his face as they entered the room. Once they were inside, he closed the door behind them with a gentle firmness that expressed his wrath more clearly than a slam ever could. Travis knew his father's moods well, and he'd wager this was the darkest of dark.

Travis positioned himself between his father and Jenna instinctively. His father would not have hurt her, but he wanted to protect her from something, maybe the embarrassment that was soon to follow.

"You two disgust me," Roland said, glaring at Travis as if he were something slimy he'd just found under a rock.

"Dad, this isn't as bad as it looks." He wanted to blurt out the truth, let his father know he wasn't the scumbag he seemed to be and that Kathryn wasn't cheating on his brother, but he held back. They'd come this far, and he couldn't ruin their plan now, even if it meant letting Kathryn look bad to his father. So long as he didn't tell Travis's mother what he'd seen, the situation could be salvaged.

He glanced over his shoulder at Jenna, whose lipstick was smudged—and probably on his face, too. There wasn't going to be any explaining away what they'd been doing in the closet. He'd simply have to bear the brunt of his father's wrath until after the wedding.

"We were just—" Jenna started, but Travis held up a hand to silence her.

"I don't want to hear your excuses."

"Dad, wait—"

"Even if I hadn't witnessed this filthy behavior, I could have guessed what's been going on. You two look at each other like a couple of dogs in heat every time you're in the same room. You could at least have the decency to be discreet."

Damn it. Travis hadn't realized how much their attraction had shown on their faces. No telling how many members of the family now considered him a no-good sleaze.

As much as his dutiful-son side wanted to protest, he kept quiet. What was the worst that could happen? Okay, his father could tell Blake what was going on and Blake could cancel the wedding. That was the consequence he had to prevent.

Jenna spoke up first, though. "I don't love Travis, Mr. Roth. I love Blake. I'm ashamed of what's happened here, and I swear it won't ever happen again."

"You're damn right it won't. I've got a mind to remove you as head of Roth Investments, Travis. Any man who behaves this way isn't fit to run a company, as far as I'm concerned."

Travis's stomach clenched into a knot. But when he tried to muster the energy to argue, nothing happened. Even stranger, the knot began to relax, as if being removed as head of Roth Investments simply wasn't that big a deal to him.

"No, you can't do that!" Jenna said. "Whatever you want—"'

"What I want is a promise from both of you that you won't go near each other again."

"Then you have my promise."

His father looked at Jenna as if her promise was about as valuable as an old shoe, but she kept her gaze leveled on him without flinching. He had to admire her courage.

"Mine, too," Travis said. "Does this mean you won't tell Blake?"

His father aimed his look of disgust at Travis again. "I should, but as far as I can tell, Blake's finally settling down with Kathryn, and I don't see any point in ruining his happiness if you two can straighten up."

Travis shouldn't have been surprised. His father would do just about anything to protect Blake. It struck him in that moment that his father's protectiveness was a big factor in Blake's irresponsibility, that having someone always looking out for him so closely had made Blake too lazy to look out for himself like an adult.

Gritting his teeth, Travis produced his most humble expression. "Thank you, Dad. I appreciate your discretion, and I don't deserve it."

"Damn right you don't. I haven't decided yet what the repercussions for you should be."

Travis glanced at Jenna and caught her stricken expression. She seemed about to protest again, but he gave her a warning look and shook his head.

So what if he had to give up Roth Investments? Was that really such a bad thing? Couldn't he find a job anywhere, doing anything he wanted? Of course he could. If his time building the family legacy had passed, Travis realized, he was okay with that. He could build his own legacy.

Roland looked back and forth between the two of them. "If I ever catch the two of you together again, you can be damn sure I'll make your lives miserable. Understand?"

They nodded simultaneously, and his father turned and stalked out of the room. Jenna exhaled and smoothed an errant curl behind her ear.

"That was fun," she whispered.

"Fun like a train wreck."

"I'm surprised he left us here alone. Do you think he's hovering in the hallway eavesdropping?"

"Anything's possible. We'd better get back to the party before anyone else comes looking for us."

"I'm so sorry, Travis."

"I'm not." He blinked at his own admission. Was it true? Yeah, it was.

Not only wasn't he sorry for letting things get out of hand with Jenna, he was damn happy that he'd finally found a woman he could feel so passionately about. If it meant losing his position at Roth Investments, screwing up his brother's wedding, failing to meet his family's expectations, so be it. He was having a hard time giving a damn.

In fact, if he had to label his predominant emotion at that moment, he'd call it…thrilled. He was falling in love with Jenna Calvert, for better or worse, and he couldn't be anything but thrilled about it.

Whether he was her type or not, he decided the

newly discovered risk taker in him would speak up and let Jenna know exactly how he felt.

But then she spoke up first.

"We have to stop. No more private encounters, no more anything."

"Because of my father?"

"Because I don't see this going anywhere, and it's only going to create more trouble the longer we mess around."

Travis absorbed the blow to his pride without flinching. Okay, so she wasn't feeling quite as adventurous as he was. That didn't mean she couldn't be persuaded. After all, he knew exactly the kind of persuasion she liked best.

"Jenna, I think what we have here is worth pursuing."

She glared at him as if he'd lost his mind. "What we have is just a sex thing."

Just a sex thing? Could he really expect her to see it as anything more when she'd entered into the relationship wanting it to be purely sexual?

No, he couldn't. And as much as he felt inspired to take a risk with her, he knew better than to push their relationship further than she wanted it to go.

"If that's the way you feel, then I guess there's nothing more to say."

"I'm sure Blake is wondering where I am by now," Jenna said, edging her way toward the door.

"Right." Travis watched as she walked out the

door, and for the first time in his life, he experienced the sensation of wanting something he couldn't have.

JENNA FLOPPED DOWN on the sofa, kicked off her heels and exhaled. She'd survived the rehearsal dinner and bachelorette party with a minimum of awkwardness. Although an alarming number of Kathryn's friends were difficult to tell apart with their identically tasteful but bland outfits and identically neutral good looks, she'd managed to keep them straight by having studied their photos.

Jenna sighed with relief. She'd survived two weeks impersonating Kathryn, and she hadn't been discovered. If it wasn't for the fact that her sister still hadn't shown up, she'd feel thrilled that tomorrow was the final day of the charade. She'd be able to take her money and go…. But then, the thought of going put a hollow feeling in her gut, as if she were leaving something behind.

Or someone.

But she couldn't leave behind a man she didn't really have any claim on, so she needed to just put that idea out of her head. She knew how to walk away with her last shed of dignity intact, and she'd do exactly that as soon as she had a check in hand.

She was just contemplating hunting down a package of chocolate chip cookies in the kitchen when her cell phone rang from inside her purse, startling her into a state of alertness. A glance at the wall clock told her it was almost midnight, and she wasn't expecting any calls. She dug the phone out of her purse.

"Hello?"

"I'm watching you," an oddly distorted voice said—the sort of voice serial killers and stalkers always used in the movies.

Jenna's stomach flip-flopped, and she glanced nervously toward the wall of windows that looked out on the ocean. Could it be that someone was lurking on the front lawn, waiting for her?

"Who is this?" she demanded.

"You'd better watch out," the voice said ominously.

It sounded like a man but could have been a woman using some kind of voice distortion device. Jenna tried to ignore the panic rising in her chest and think what she should do next.

"Watch out for what?"

And then she heard nothing but silence. The caller had hung up. Jenna's mouth went dry, and she hit the end call button and dropped the phone as if it had caught fire.

Had her stalker caught up with her in Carmel? If so, how? Was he watching her from outside?

The thought made her grab the phone again to call 911. But then she remembered the detective who was working on her case in the city. Should she call him first?

No, she decided. She needed to call the local police first, have someone come out and look around. But rather than find the phone book to look up the nonemergency police number, she could only think of Travis's number, which she'd already managed to memorize in the short time she'd known him.

She was just about to dial it when the doorbell rang.

Jenna's breath caught in her throat. She glanced around for a weapon and realized she had nothing. She'd let her guard down since coming to Carmel; she'd felt safe.

A small, abstract marble sculpture sat on a nearby table. Jenna picked it up and felt the weight of it in her hands. It could do serious damage if it made contact with the right body part.

She crept to the door and peered out the peephole, half expecting to see a thug in a ski mask.

Instead, she saw Blake, which was almost as bad as a thug in a ski mask. It occurred to her only then that a criminal probably wouldn't have bothered to ring the doorbell. Tension drained from her body, and she expelled a pent-up breath she hadn't realized she'd been holding in.

Jenna considered just not opening the door, but no sooner did the thought form in her head than Blake peered in the window beside the door and saw her standing there.

Damn it.

She turned the lock and slowly opened the door. "Hey, baby. I just had to see you again tonight," he said, but "just" came out sounding like "jush," and his eyes looked bleary.

"Have you been drinking?"

"Jush a little bit. Are you gonna make me stand out here in the cold all night?"

Jenna peered out at the driveway. No car. "How did you get here?"

"I got a ride with a couple of guys from the bachelor party."

She didn't see any choice but to step aside and let him in. He gave her a crooked smile and shuffled into the living room.

"They wanted to go to a strip club," he continued, "but I told them that if I saw any naked women tonight, it was going to be my own woman."

"Oh. How…sweet." Jenna's mouth went dry, and she tried to produce on a nonpanicked smile. "But don't forget our agreement."

"It's less than a day until the wedding. I'm dying here!"

"Exactly—less than a day. By tomorrow night, we'll be…" What? If Kathryn failed to show up, would they be married and stuck in conjugal bliss? Jenna forced herself not to shudder. "Married."

Blake flashed another bleary smile and weaved toward her, his arms extended in a clumsy hug. He nearly toppled Jenna. "Come on baby, please?"

He found her ear and jammed his tongue into it, and the overture made her think of being assaulted by a slug.

Jenna untangled herself from his embrace and stepped back, resisting the urge to rub her ear. "Blakey, you've clearly had too much to drink, and if you don't sleep it off, you're going to feel awful for our wedding."

"Can I sleep here?"

"If I see you in the morning, it will be bad luck."

"But I don't have a way home."

So she'd call him a cab—but that sounded like a pretty coldhearted thing for Kathryn to offer. Jenna just wanted to get out of this place, away from this man, out of her sister's life.

"I'll drive you home."

Blake seemed to be trying to figure out how his plan to get laid had gone wrong. He frowned. "But…"

"Don't worry, darling," she forced out, "we'll be together tomorrow. Tonight, we both need our rest."

"Um…"

Jenna found her shoes and grabbed her keys and purse. "Come on, let's go before we change our minds and do something stupid."

Like ditch Blake on the side of the road.

She brushed past him and marched out to Kathryn's car, then climbed into the driver's seat and watched as her faux fiancé shuffled to the car like a forlorn puppy.

He was just acting like a typical guy who couldn't understand why his fiancée was behaving so strangely. She was directing her anger at the wrong person. Truly, the only person she had to be angry with was herself for agreeing to impersonate her sister. She needed to cut Blake some slack. Aside from his inability to hold his alcohol and his generally airheaded view of life, he was a decent guy, a good match for Kathryn.

Why that suddenly mattered to her, she couldn't say, but it struck her then how oddly close to her twin she felt after walking around in her life for a few weeks. It was almost as if she were starting to miss Kathryn.

Miss Kathryn? No way.

Blake settled into the passenger seat and emitted periodic yawns as Jenna drove. She reached for the radio to avoid any further conversation, but as soon as she found a station, Blake turned it off.

"It's kinda strange. Sometimes I feel like you're becoming a different person."

Jenna stiffened, and her palms grew damp on the steering wheel. "How so?"

"Like that radio station. You never used to like talk radio. You said it made your head hurt."

Oh, right. "I'm just trying to expand my horizons—that's all." She tilted her head in that cutesy way Kathryn always did. "I want to be able to impress your friends with my knowledge of world events and stuff."

"Honey, you don't need to worry about impressing my friends."

"Well, if you say so..."

"It's not just the radio thing. It's the way you've

seemed a little standoffish in the past few weeks, and you've had this look in your eyes."

"What kind of look?"

He seemed to search for the right words. "Like you're always thinking of the punch line to a dirty joke."

Jenna glanced at herself in the rearview mirror. *Did* she always have that look in her eyes?

"I guess it's just prewedding jitters."

"It's almost like you're a whole new woman since you came back from that spa."

Jenna focused on the road ahead and did her best to keep from steering off into a ditch. Travis would have choked to hear his little brother making such astute observations.

"Well, my week there had quite an impact on me." In a manner of speaking.

"You haven't had any second thoughts about the wedding, have you?"

"Don't be silly, darling. I can't wait until tomorrow." At least that much was true. Come Saturday night, she hoped to be long gone from Carmel, no longer walking around in Kathryn's life.

Or she could be stuck in a fake marriage with her sister's intended.

Jenna steered into Blake's driveway and left the engine idling, waiting for Blake to get the heck out of her car. She looked at him expectantly, but he didn't budge.

"Only a matter of hours, and we'll be married!" She forced a smile and an affectionate pat on the arm.

Blake leaned over to kiss her, and she offered up her right cheek.

"Well, see you at the wedding tomorrow, then."

When he'd stumbled inside his front door, Jenna backed out of the driveway and found herself dreading the thought of returning to Kathryn's place again. She made a left instead of a right at the first intersection she came to, taking her away from Kathryn's house and toward...what?

She wanted the fastest escape route out of Kathryn's life, and the only person in Carmel who knew her as Jenna and therefore could provide that escape wasn't likely to welcome her with open arms. Ever since their encounter in the coat closet and subsequent confrontation with Roland Roth, Travis had been cool and distant, and she couldn't blame him.

She felt horrible that his relationship with his father and his entire plan to help her sister was in jeopardy just because she couldn't keep her hands off him, and she didn't want to make matters any worse than they already were. She'd sworn to herself that night that she wouldn't touch Travis again, that she wouldn't so much as look in his direction.

But as she steered Kathryn's convertible onto the main road through town, her destination became clear. She needed to talk to him, to see him, like she needed air and water. It was surely just the stress of dealing with Blake again so late at night, but a magnetic force pulled her toward the one destination she should have avoided at all costs.

Travis may not welcome her, but she had to try. She had to have someone look at her and see her true self, even if it was only long enough to tell her to get lost. If she could just be Jenna, even for only a few minutes, then maybe she could sleep tonight.

Ten minutes later, she parked in the space next to Travis's Mercedes. When she reached his door, her hands grew clammy, and she had to wipe them off on her dress. At this late hour, a few lights were still on in Travis's condo. She took a deep breath and rang the doorbell.

When he opened the door, his expression was neutral. "Is something wrong?"

"Blake came by tonight drunk to beg his fiancée to come to her senses and sleep with him."

"What did you do?"

"I drove him home. What did you think? I'd invite him in for a roll in the hay?"

"I didn't say that. Are you okay?"

"It just shook me up a little. I'm not even sure why I'm here."

His expression still blank, he stepped aside. "Come in."

Jenna stopped in the foyer, wondering what the hell she was doing. Hoping for another night with him? In spite of their differences, in spite of the fact that they couldn't be caught together, in spite of the fact that they had no basis for a real relationship?

Had she gotten that desperate? She took one look at the expanse of his shoulders in a white oxford and knew that she had. She wanted him, regardless of everything else.

She hugged herself, suddenly feeling chilly. A rush of emotion hit her in the chest, and she felt her eyes welling up with tears.

What the hell was going on here? Jenna Calvert didn't burst into tears at the slightest sign of stress.

That was the sort of thing her sister would do. Was she turning into Kathryn after spending two weeks in her life?

Hell no. She blinked away the tears and forced herself to smile. "I'm fine," she said, but her voice broke on "fine."

Travis took her into his arms and held her close, letting the heat of his chest warm her. She slid her arms around his waist and allowed herself to sink in and savor the feel of him. So what if she was crying like a helpless damsel in distress?

Travis pulled back and tilted her face up to his. "I've missed this."

This, as in their physical relationship. Not her. Still, it was something.

"So have I."

She watched his internal struggle reveal itself in his eyes. She'd have bet anything he was trying to decide how far he would allow himself to go.

"You know the first time we kissed, in the parking lot of that biker bar?"

"Yes."

"I felt like a new man that night. How is it that you have such a strong effect on me?"

"I don't know. Is that a good thing or a bad thing?"

"I don't know, either."

"I guess you have to decide if you want to be the kind of guy who makes out in the parking lot of a biker bar," she said, only half joking.

"I guess so," he murmured right before placing a soft kiss on her lips.

Jenna held back, letting him decide how far to take it. And he did nothing more than brush his lips on hers. But that barely there sensation was like electricity, bringing all her nerve endings to life.

"I didn't come here for this," she whispered.

"Then why did you come here?"

"Because you know I'm not Kathryn."

"It will all be over with tomorrow." He brushed a strand of hair off her cheek.

"Will it? What if Kathryn doesn't show up? Have you even heard from her?"

He paled. "Not since Monday. I was sure I'd convinced her she can't miss her own wedding."

"But I know Kathryn. If she doesn't look perfect, she's not going to show. Was her face still swollen on Monday?"

Travis nodded, his expression grim.

Jenna shuddered. The thought of really having to go through with a fraudulent wedding was something she hadn't allowed herself to consider much. "Does the minister know he might not be performing a legal ceremony?"

Travis exhaled and walked over to the couch, where he collapsed and raked his fingers through his hair. He looked exhausted. "I explained to him that the bride and groom might not be prepared to sign the marriage certificate tomorrow."

That still didn't eliminate the problem of standing at a church altar and making false vows. Jenna knew without a doubt that, regardless of the twenty-five grand, she couldn't do *that*. Masquerading as her sister for the sake of a good cause was one thing, but playing games with the divine was more than Jenna was willing to do.

"Travis, if she doesn't show up—"

He held up a hand. "Let's don't cross that bridge unless we have to."

Right. She didn't have the energy to push the issue now, so she'd just keep blindly hoping, at least until morning, that Kathryn would show.

Jenna slipped off her sandals and went to the couch, then sat down beside Travis, releasing a sigh she hadn't realized had built up inside her. He reached out and ran his thumb along the edge of her jaw, a gentle caress that said more than words could have.

All her good intentions melted away, and she wanted him with a fierceness that wouldn't be denied.

"You look like you're in need of some stress relief," she whispered.

His weary expression transformed into a slow smile. "You'd better believe it."

That was all the invitation she needed. She climbed onto his lap, well aware that the maneuver pushed the skirt of her dress up to the tops of her thighs. If he wanted, he'd get a prime view of her hot pink lace panties.

His hands found her bare thighs, and he slid them up until his fingertips brushed the seam of her panties. "I was hoping you'd come over here."

"What else are you hoping for?"

"You probably know that better than I do."

Jenna leaned in and brushed his lips with the lightest of kisses. "I think I've got a pretty good idea."

11

THERE WAS NO DENYING how much Travis wanted Jenna. No more playing games, no more ignoring the electricity that surged between them. At least not tonight.

The moment he'd seen her on his doorstep, he knew he had to have her one more time. Maybe the morning light would reveal all the ugly truths that kept them apart, but for tonight, there was no further will left in him to resist her wild sex appeal. Even all polished up as a duplicate of Kathryn, Jenna was still an untamable vixen. He'd been a fool to think he could change that—a fool to have ever wanted to change her.

She began to unbuckle his belt, and a moment later her hand slipped inside his pants and found him hard and ready. He lifted her up from the couch and all but dragged her to the bedroom, where he pinned her on the bed and pushed her dress up to her waist, suddenly feeling that same caveman rush he'd first experienced at the biker bar.

With Jenna, he wasn't Travis Roth the CEO, or the dutiful son, or the wealthy catch. He was someone entirely different—someone he wasn't quite sure he recognized as himself, at least not before two weeks ago. Jenna seemed oblivious to his money, unimpressed with his status, interested in him purely as a man.

Travis trailed hungry kisses up her leg until he found the sensitive flesh of her inner thigh. He took a gentle bite, then moved up to her panties and tugged at them with his teeth. Once he'd rid her of the hot pink scrap of lace, he buried his face in her honey-colored curls and plunged his tongue inside her.

She bucked and gasped, but he held her hips still as he began to massage and explore with his tongue. Soon, she settled in and let him do as he pleased.

When her breathing became rapid and shallow, he pulled back, not wanting her to leave satisfied too soon—not when he had so many other things he wanted to do with her yet. He crawled up onto her and settled his hips between her legs, then began to grind through the fabric of his underwear. She was wet and ready for him, and the sensation of it, even through cotton, was amazing.

He didn't want any barriers now, though. He wanted to feel her hot flesh warming his whole body, so he stood and pulled her up by her hands, then freed her of her dress and bra. It only took another few moments for him to get undressed himself and reposition himself between her legs. He wanted so badly to be buried in the wet heat of her that he nearly forgot himself, but just in time, he remembered the need for a condom and reached for his nightstand drawer to find one.

Once he'd tugged it on, Jenna wrapped her legs tight around his waist and with a shift of her hips, he slid inside of her. He pushed himself deeper until their bodies were completely joined, and then he paused and buried his face in her neck, savoring the feel of her.

Jenna slid her hands down his back and grasped his buttocks as she sank her teeth into his shoulder, and he could no longer lie still. He raised up on his elbows and thrust into her with growing intensity, watching pleasure transform her face as she gasped and cried out.

This was where he belonged, where he fit perfectly, where he never wanted to leave. Here with Jenna, just the two of them, Travis felt as if he'd found his place in the world—or at least his place in bed.

He paused long enough to taste her breasts, savoring the heavy, perfect weight of them, her tight nipples begging for his attention. He inhaled her soft, female scent and committed it to memory, because he knew he'd need something to cling to after she walked out of his life.

Wrapping his arms around her, he rolled onto his back and pulled Jenna on top of him. When she sat up and began rocking her hips, the sensation brought him instantly to the edge of climax, until he willed his body to slow down. He grasped her hips and slowed her pace, savoring each shift of her body against him.

She watched him as they made love, her gaze as bold as everything else about her, but for the first time, watching her, too, Travis noticed something in her gaze he'd never seen before—vulnerability. Peering out from behind the untamable temptress, he saw a woman who wasn't totally sure of something.

But then she grasped his wrists and pinned them over his head, increasing their pace on her own, driving them quickly toward release. And when she began to cry out, her contractions brought him his release, too. He broke free from the binds of her hands and pulled her against him, kissed her long and hard until the waves of pleasure passed.

In that moment, with Jenna in his arms, Travis knew that what they had was a once-in-a-lifetime kind of connection, and he could not imagine letting her go.

JENNA AWOKE to the sensation of a man's warm body against hers, and she realized with a start that she'd allowed herself to fall asleep in Travis's bed. She looked around for a clock and saw one on the nightstand that said it was 5:00 a.m.

Damn it, she'd never intended to stay here all night, and she wanted to leave before anyone might stop by and see Kathryn's car parked in Travis's driveway.

She sat up and watched Travis for a moment as he slept. Heat radiated out from his body, warming her, reminding her of the heat they'd generated earlier. Together, they were combustible, and she couldn't imagine recreating such chemistry with another man.

But there would be no more nights like this with Travis. He'd hired her to impersonate her sister, and the fact that she'd slept with him, too, was just a perk to him. An unexpected benefit.

So, that was life. She wasn't going to get all bent out of shape just because some millionaire bachelor wanted her sexually.

That's all she'd wanted from him, too, wasn't it?

Absolutely.

"Something wrong?" Travis said, his voice gravelly from sleep.

"I'd better go. I've got an early day today, and so do you."

"The wedding," he groaned. "Don't remind me." He rolled toward her and draped his arm across her lap. "You don't have to leave."

"What if Blake shows up here in a few hours— what if anyone does?"

"Oh, right." His voice was stronger now. He'd been jarred wide awake at the thought of their getting caught, apparently.

Jenna slipped out from under the weight of his arm and stood up from the bed, oddly uncomfortable with her nakedness for the first time in front of Travis. She groped around on the floor for her clothes and fumbled to dress quickly in the half darkness.

"I guess we'll see each other at the wedding, then."

He sat up in bed and exhaled a frustrated sigh. "I'm sure it won't come to that."

"How can you be so sure when you haven't even heard from Kathryn?"

"If she doesn't show up, the wedding is off."

Jenna paused in the middle of zipping her dress. "After all the trouble you've gone through, you'd really let it be called off?"

"I won't let you participate in a fraudulent wedding."

"Oh." She'd never expected him to put her above his family now, after they'd gone through so much trouble to cover for Kathryn.

He slipped out of bed himself and tugged on a pair of pants, then went to his dresser. "In case I don't get a chance later, I should pay you now."

Jenna watched, her throat and mouth going dry as he withdrew a check from his wallet and strode over to her.

"Twenty-five thousand dollars, as we agreed upon."

She stared at the check, at his small, neat handwriting that spelled out the numbers to more money than she'd ever been given at one time. She should have been happy to have her money and a one-way ticket out of Kathryn's life, but instead, she finally saw exactly what she'd gotten herself into.

Standing there with her dress half-zipped in Travis's bedroom, with his scent still lingering on her skin, she understood what she was to him.

A whore.

She'd been his paid distraction for a few stressful weeks, and she'd walked right into the job willingly. She'd even volunteered her services—made them a part of the deal.

Her voice caught in her throat, and she couldn't lift her hand to take the check. Wouldn't take it. She still had one last scrap of her pride, at least, and she could use it to walk out of Travis's life now and for good.

Blinking back tears, she shook her head. "Keep your damn money."

Jenna turned and hurried from the room, grabbed her bag in the living room and found her shoes. Travis stopped her at the front door.

"What's the matter?"

"Your timing couldn't be more clear. You don't have to pay me off to make sure I get lost."

He looked at her as if she were speaking a foreign language. "You held up your end of the deal, and you earned the money."

"I'm not a prostitute."

"I never said you were." He reached out for her, but she skirted his touch. "You were the one who suggested we bring sex into the deal."

"Right. It was the stupidest idea I've ever had." She opened the door and ran out, determined not to let him see her tears.

"Jenna, wait!"

But she didn't. She climbed into Kathryn's car and slammed the door, tossing Travis a look that let him know exactly how bad an idea it would be to follow her.

Of all the wild stunts she'd ever pulled in the face of stress, sleeping with Travis Roth had been, by far, the dumbest, and now she only wanted to get as far away from him as possible. Maybe distance would ease her sense of foolishness. Or not. At the very least, running away gave her something to do.

Jenna was halfway back to Kathryn's house when she glanced into the rearview mirror and noted the pair of headlights that had been with her, she was almost sure, nearly since she'd left Travis's condo. If she hadn't been so focused on making sure he didn't follow her, she might not have noticed this car.

As she navigated the roads through town, tension coiled inside her the longer the car stayed on her tail. It would have been an amazing coincidence for someone to be out driving so early in the morning, taking the exact same path through town that Jenna was taking.

But why would anyone follow her? Could it have been Blake, suspicious of his fiancée having an affair, now ready to confront her with proof? Jenna chewed her lip, imagining what she might say if confronted. Now that she'd turned down Travis's money, would she just tell Blake the truth, or would she leave that for Travis and Kathryn to explain? Maybe they were the ones who deserved to face Blake's wrath.

But what if it wasn't Blake? What if the person or persons who'd been after her in San Francisco *had* tracked her down in sleepy little Carmel? What if they were just waiting for the opportunity to run her off the road—or worse?

To test the theory, she took a few unnecessary turns and watched as the car followed her. Her heart raced, and she began scanning the street for a police station, a fire station—anyplace safe. All she spotted was a twenty-four hour gas station lit up in the fading early morning darkness. It would have to do. Jenna pulled into it and parked, then watched as the car slowed in front of the station and continued on down the road. Jenna couldn't see more than an outline of the driver, but if she'd had to guess, she would have said it was a woman.

The car was a sedan bland enough that she couldn't tell the make or model, definitely not Blake's splashy red Porsche.

Maybe she was just letting paranoia get the best of her. Who could have tracked her down here? Really, the notion of someone following her all the way to Carmel, lurking in the shadows undetected the entire time, was preposterous.

Inch by inch the tension drained from her body as she watched the car's taillights travel farther and farther away, then disappear completely. It really had just been an odd coincidence that the car had made all the same turns as Jenna. Maybe the person had been lost and was just following the only other car on the road hoping to find his or her way back to the center of town.

Yes, that had to be it. Jenna exhaled a ragged breath and pulled out of the gas station lot.

12

JENNA AWOKE WITH A START, her brain groggy from too little sleep. The alarm clock confirmed that it was only 9:00 a.m.—three hours since she'd collapsed in bed.

She was aware of the sensation of someone's presence in the room. But she wasn't at Travis's house anymore, so she should have been alone. She sat up in bed, her heart pounding, and nearly screamed when she saw a figure sitting at the foot of the bed.

It took her a split second to realize it was her twin sister. "Kathryn!"

"Hey, sis. Nice hair." Kathryn smiled, and Jenna noted that there were no unsightly bulges on her lips or cheeks.

"Your face is normal," she muttered, pushing herself up in bed and squinting at her sister in the morning sunlight.

Perfectly normal, if slightly more inflated than what nature had given them.

Kathryn lifted a hand to her cheek self-consciously. "The swelling only went down completely yesterday."

"You could have called to let us know you were coming back."

"I'm sorry. I tried, but I couldn't reach Travis. I figured you would know I wouldn't miss my own wedding."

"We couldn't be sure about that."

"I missed my flight home last night because of traffic on the way to the airport, so I had to catch the red-eye this morning."

"I'm just glad you're back. I couldn't have gone through with a sham wedding," she said, remembering only after she spoke that Travis had relieved her of that responsibility.

She forced the memory of early morning out of her head.

"Thank you...for everything. I know it probably seems ridiculous to you, but—"

"But you want your in-laws and everyone else to think well of you."

Kathryn blinked at her lack of hostility. "Yes."

"That's understandable."

"Um, thanks."

It struck Jenna that this was possibly the longest and most civil conversation she'd had with her sister in years. Strangely, she didn't even feel like throttling Kathryn for nearly missing her own wedding and putting Jenna through two weeks of the most bizarre sort of torture.

She yawned and stretched. Time to start getting ready for the wedding—that is, it would be if she were still the bride. Which she wasn't, thank God.

The thought thrilled her so much, she nearly leaped out of bed to give her sister a big hug. Instead, she swung her legs over the edge and sat there until the fog lifted from her brain.

"It must have been strange for you, pretending to be me, walking around in my life."

Jenna tried to muster some righteous anger, or at least a sense of annoyance, but nothing came. Walking around in her sister's life for two weeks had made her...what? Want Kathryn back in her life, she realized with a start.

She didn't want them to be separated by petty differences anymore. She wanted a sister. The Roths, for all their problems, clearly benefited from having such a close family, and Jenna had started to understand what she'd been missing out on by letting her differences with her twin get in the way of their relationship.

"It was definitely strange..." she said, staring across the room at the little music box Kathryn had had since they were kids. Jenna knew that if she opened it, a ballerina would pop up and start spinning around as tinkling music played. She'd had an identical one long ago.

"Travis said you were able to handle Blake without any incidents." Jenna looked over at Kathryn to see her staring at her hopefully.

"Don't worry, there was no hanky-panky. He thinks you read a sex manual at the spa that convinced you of the value of no physical contact for the two weeks leading up to the wedding."

Kathryn laughed. "Poor guy. I wish Travis would have let me tell him what was going on, but he was convinced Blake wouldn't be able to keep up the act if he knew you weren't me. He was probably right."

"Blake showed up here last night, drunk and ready for action. You drove him home."

"Oh. Thanks."

"Are you going to tell him about this whole thing?"

"Of course. I think I'll wait until the honeymoon, though, so the news doesn't upset our wedding day."

"How do you think he'll take it?"

Kathryn smiled. "I'm sure he'll take the news just fine if I time it well—say, when he's basking in the afterglow of reunion sex."

"That's all the detail I need."

"I feel awful getting married with a lie between us, though."

"Maybe you should tell him now." Jenna stood up and stretched her back, feeling the tension drain away bit by bit as the reality that she no longer had to be Kathryn sunk in.

"I don't know...."

"I think he'll take it okay. So long as you tell him why you did what you did, he'll understand."

"You think?"

"I'm sure. Maybe you could bring him some breakfast and coffee to help him with his hangover."

Kathryn stood up from the bed. "I'd better get

going then. I don't have much time before I have to be at the salon."

"I guess I'll hang out here if you don't mind. I don't have a way home—"

"You'll come to the wedding, won't you?"

"I'm invited?"

Jenna imagined having to see Travis again, and her stomach grew queasy.

"Of course." Kathryn gave her an odd look. "I was hoping the fact that you were willing to help me meant we could stop being mad at each other."

"Yeah, me, too."

"I'm sorry, Jen. I didn't treat you well in high school, and it's only gotten worse since then."

"I didn't make it easy to be nice."

"I guess I had my own resentments for the way you wanted to be different from me. I'd always loved the way things were when we were 'the twins.'"

"I know you did." Jenna had a sudden and uncontrollable urge to hug her sister for the first time in more years than she could remember. Maybe she'd never enjoyed being one of an inseparable pair the way Kathryn had, but she could understand her sister's longings, at least.

She went to Kathryn and gave her an awkward squeeze. Her sister smiled when they parted, and Jenna felt silly for having to blink back the sudden dampness in her eyes.

"Now go talk to that fiancé of yours. I'll be here when you get back."

"You promise?"

"I promise."

Jenna watched as Kathryn hurried out the door, her designer sundress swishing as she walked, and she realized for once that she was looking at her sister and not just her identical twin.

TRAVIS DOUBLE-CHECKED his pocket for the wedding ring, then headed out into the church lobby to greet the guests who were beginning to trickle in. Kathryn had said Jenna was going to attend the wedding, but that didn't mean she'd even give him a cold glance.

Not that he could blame her. His timing had been lousy, trying to offer her a check right after she'd climbed out of his bed, but he wouldn't feel right until he knew she was compensated for all the trouble she'd gone through.

Travis smiled and nodded at distant relations and acquaintances as he wandered through the lobby. It wasn't until the church was half-full that he spotted the tall, slender blonde he'd been looking for. She wore a racy red dress that set her apart from her sister, and she'd done something to her hair that had transformed it from Kathryn's classic, tasteful style to a wild, sexy mop of waves and spikes. Her lips were painted vixen-red to match her dress, and her high-heeled sandals were the exact same shade.

Here was the woman who'd invited him into her shower, who'd seduced him in a biker bar, who'd turned him from an uptight bore into a man he could hardly recognize as himself. A man who took risks at work and in his personal life and felt exhilarated by each and every one of them.

But seeing Jenna gave him a stab of regret, as if he'd failed in taking a risk where it mattered most.

She climbed the steps of the church and entered the front doors without so much as glancing at him.

"Jenna?"

She shot him a look of pure animosity, her eyes icy blue. And then she kept walking, straight into the sanctuary, where she found a seat in one of the rear pews.

Others had noticed her, too, and were staring after her in disbelief. "Was that—" a man standing next to Travis began.

"That was Kathryn's twin sister, Jenna."

"I had no idea she had a twin."

"They're not very close," Travis said before wandering away.

His father caught up with him. "Travis, was that Kathryn's sister?"

"Yes," he said, trying to make his way back to the sanctuary where it was almost time for him to take his place at the altar next to Blake.

"Something strange is going on here." His father eyed him with interest, giving the matter serious thought. "Why do I get the feeling you have some explaining to do?"

"I have to go, Dad."

"There's been something odd about Kathryn these past few weeks, hasn't there?"

"In what way?"

"She just hasn't seemed like herself. And I never would have pegged her as an adulterer until I saw it with my own eyes...."

It took all his willpower not to confess the truth.

"Do you have something you need to tell me, son?"

"I'm not sure what you're talking about," he lied.

"Whatever it is, you've got my word I'll keep quiet about it."

Travis exhaled all of his frustration and pulled his dad to the side. "Kathryn disappeared, okay? She went off to a spa and had some botched lip enhancements done, then refused to come home. I hired her twin sister to impersonate her."

There. Now Roland Roth would know exactly how big a control freak his elder son really was.

But instead of looking disgusted, his father grinned. "You went to all that trouble to keep this wedding on track?"

He nodded.

"Blake couldn't have been in on this—he's too lousy at keeping a secret."

"He had no idea."

"But how did you keep him from coming on to the wrong woman?"

"Jenna took care of that. She kept him at arm's length the entire time."

And then a look of understanding dawned on

his father's face. "So I didn't catch you and *Kathryn* fooling around—it was you and her sister!"

In spite of himself, Travis felt a huge burden lifted from his shoulders. He realized then that no matter how badly he wanted not to care what his father thought of him, he did.

"Exactly."

"I'll make sure your mother never hears about this."

"Thanks, Dad. Now we'd better find our places."

The lobby had emptied, and everyone was seated inside the church now. He was supposed to be at the front of the sanctuary with Blake.

Travis found Blake in the rest room, adjusting his bow tie and patting nervously at his hair in a mirror. "It's time for us to go out."

"Kathryn talked to me today."

"About?"

Blake tossed him a look through the mirror. "You know what about. You could have told me."

"Could I? You're sure you could have kept quiet?"

Blake's expression turned sheepish. "Okay, probably not. But still, it weirds me out to know I was hitting on Kathryn's sister."

"Sorry."

Blake turned away from the mirror and gave Travis a friendly clap on the shoulder. "Thank you for helping Kathryn out the way you did. I know how important it was to her to keep Mom and

Dad and everyone else from thinking badly of her, and you kept the charity project on track."

Travis glanced at his watch again. "We'd better get going."

A few moments later they were positioned at the altar, and as Travis looked out over the crowd, he couldn't help letting his gaze settle on Jenna. She, however, never looked back at him.

And then his attention was drawn away from Jenna to a woman who entered the back of the church and looked around nervously. She was wearing a blue dress and clutching a matching blue handbag to her side as if it contained the crown jewels. Something about her seemed...off. Not quite right. Travis felt himself tense as he watched her.

She scanned the crowd from left to right, then took a seat near the end of the last pew. Jenna noticed the woman then, too, and stared at her with a look of recognition before looking away.

Travis relaxed then. The woman must have been someone Jenna and Kathryn knew.

Music began to play, and Kathryn's maid of honor started down the aisle. Next came the procession of identically lavender-satin-clad brides-maids, then the flower girl. Finally, the music transitioned into the bridal march, and everyone in the church stood and turned to watch the bride enter.

Kathryn started down the aisle with her step-father accompanying her, but again Travis found his gaze wandering away from the bride to her sister. Jenna was staring at the woman in the blue dress again, and he watched in what felt like slow motion as the woman reached into her handbag and withdrew a small handgun, then aimed it at Kathryn with shaking hands.

"Stop! A gun!" he yelled as his feet sprang into motion and carried him down the aisle.

But Jenna had seen the gun, too, and she pushed her way past people until there was no one between her and the woman with the weapon. She tackled the woman, and they were scrambling on the ground when Travis reached the back of the church and pushed his way through the gathering crowd.

The gun fired, and it felt as if his heart stopped beating. There was a collective pause, and then an uproar as someone shouted, "She's been shot! Call an ambulance!"

When Travis spotted Jenna on the floor, she was curled up in a fetal position with blood oozing from her side. His pulse kicked into overdrive, and he raced to her and dropped to his knees beside her.

He was vaguely aware of several men subduing the woman in the blue dress while she howled for them to let go of her. As he gently placed a hand on Jenna's shoulder, the crowd milled about them, and someone called out for a doctor.

"Jenna? Can you hear me?"

She said nothing. He felt for a pulse in her neck and was relieved to feel a faint but steady one. His throat tightened up, then his chest. He didn't want to lose her. Doing the only thing he could think of, he took off his jacket and pressed it to the wound on her side.

More than anything else in the world, he wanted her safe and well. He would have done anything to see her well again.

The sound of a woman's hysterical sobbing caught his attention, and he looked up to see Kathryn nearby, Blake restraining her, trying to console her.

"I'll take a look at her," a familiar voice said.

Travis looked up to see Bob Jensen, a surgeon and an old family friend, kneeling beside Jenna. He began examining her as she lay limp and unconscious, the bloodstain on her dress growing in spite of Travis's efforts.

"Is she going to be okay?"

"I don't know."

His eyes stung as he tried not to think about what "I don't know" might mean.

If he had the chance, he would make things right between them. And if he didn't have the chance, he'd spend the rest of his life regretting it.

JENNA STRUGGLED to climb out of the hazy nothingness. She heard voices, and images flashed in her mind. The woman in the brown wig, the gun, the explosive sound, the searing pain in her side. She didn't want to die.

Her eyes opened, and there was light, but she

couldn't focus. Her mind couldn't wrap itself around one thought for more than a moment. Was this what dying felt like?

"Jenna?" A voice sliced through her fear and gave her something to struggle toward.

Travis. She wanted to cry out with relief that he was there, but the haze wouldn't lift. She listened for his voice and fought to form complete thoughts. At least, she understood, she was alive.

Her last memory was of the woman in the brown wig, the woman who'd seemed oddly familiar until she aimed the gun at Kathryn, and then Jenna had known who she was.

Finally, she could open her eyes again, and she saw Travis. He looked as if he'd been awake for days, with dark half moons under his eyes and a five o'clock shadow coloring his jaw. His bow tie was gone, his tuxedo shirtsleeves rolled up, the formerly pristine white fabric splattered with blood.

Her blood.

His gaze was locked on Jenna, and she felt all the air whoosh out of her lungs. She hadn't realized how badly she'd wanted to see him, how much of the aching inside her had been a longing for him to be at her side. So much for her resolve not to let emotions get involved.

She struggled to clear her mind of the fog, to keep her eyes focused and thoughts coherent. Slowly, the fog lifted.

"Do you feel up to having a visitor?"

She tried to produce a smile. "Maybe just one,"

she said and was surprised when the words came out fully formed.

"Good." He stood up from his chair and gingerly sat down on the edge of her bed. "I was afraid you'd kick me out as soon as you saw me."

Jenna tried to sit up in bed, but the pain in her side convinced her that a horizontal position wasn't so bad. Then she noticed the buttons that raised and lowered the bed, and in a matter of seconds she'd adjusted the bed to a gentle angle just short of causing the pain to worsen.

He took her hand in his. "Hey, you. How are you feeling?"

"I've been better. I guess I ruined Kathryn's wedding."

"You didn't ruin anything. Everyone's waiting to hear that you're okay. They're planning to finish the ceremony tonight."

"The woman who shot me—was she caught?"

He nodded. "She's in police custody now. Apparently she's someone you interviewed during your research of the pageant industry?"

"I recognized her when I saw her in the church, but it took me a little too long to put two and two together. She'd been at your parents' Fourth of July party, too, but the wig she was wearing threw me."

"She's the one who's been harassing you, isn't she?"

"That's my guess. She seemed a little disturbed by my questions when I interviewed her, but I wrote it off as her not wanting to cast the pageant industry in a bad light. Today she must have gotten Kathryn mixed up with me."

"I don't understand how she could have confused the two of you, unless she knew about your impersonating Kathryn."

Jenna thought of the car that had followed her the night before. "Maybe she's been following us ever since you picked me up in San Francisco."

"Why wait until the wedding to make her move?"

Jenna shrugged, feeling just as perplexed as Travis looked.

"I'll call the police station later to see what they can tell us about her motives, if anything. But for now," he took her hand in his, "we have more important matters to discuss."

Jenna remembered then how her life had become condensed into a ten-second movie in the short time between her being shot and passing out. Everything that had been confusing and uncertain prior to the bullet entering her torso had suddenly become simple issues of black and white. She understood that whatever petty differences had created a rift between herself and Travis, she should have worked to get past them.

She should have known that the most powerful attraction to any man she'd ever felt was something not to be ignored. And she should have recognized the emotions Travis evoked in her as exactly what they were—love.

If getting shot in the side had convinced her of anything, it was never to let a chance for true love slip through her fingers.

"Yes, we do," she said.

Jenna struggled to move herself closer to Travis, wincing at the pain that throbbed in her side.

"You shouldn't try to move yet."

She crooked her finger at him. "Come a little closer then."

Travis carefully stretched out in the bed beside her and propped his head on his elbow next to her. "Close enough?"

"I love you," she whispered.

He traced a fingertip along her jawline. "I never want to feel like I've lost you again."

"And?" Jenna was going to muster her last ounce of strength to kick him out of her bed if he didn't return her feelings.

He smiled. "I love you, Jenna. I love everything about you—your wildness, your intelligence, your beauty, your strength…. I love the way you make me feel like a more adventurous man, and I don't ever want to go back to the way I used to feel."

She blinked at the dampness in her eyes. Her throat constricted, and she couldn't think of a single reply that would do his words justice.

"I've got a proposition for you," he said before she could speak.

"I think I've had more than one lifetime's worth of your business propositions," she said, her stomach turning queasy at the thought of what he might say next.

"This isn't business, it's personal, and don't worry, I've learned my lesson."

"What lesson, exactly, did you learn?" Jenna asked.

"To never, ever try to tame a wild vixen like you into a proper society lady."

"Ah, that's probably good for you to know."

"So do you want to hear my proposal?"

"I'm listening."

"What do you say the next wedding we attend be our own?"

Jenna's heart got stuck in her throat, but after a moment she managed to say, "Are you asking me to marry you?"

"I am."

Nothing had ever been so clear to her as the fact that she and Travis belonged together, that she was complete with him in a way that she could never be without him. None of their external differences mattered.

"I'll do it on one condition...."

"If it's anything like the condition you placed on our last deal, I think I can accommodate you."

"Oh yeah? You want to have another weekend of sensual stress relief with me?"

"No."

"How about a week, then?"

"Definitely not acceptable."

"A month?"

"Not even close."

Jenna pulled him closer and silenced him with a kiss.

He pulled back just enough to say, "I want an unlimited, lifetime guarantee of Jenna Calvert-style stress relief."

She smiled at her future husband. "I think you've got yourself a deal."

Epilogue

Maui, three months later...

TRAVIS SQUINTED as his eyes adjusted to the dimly lit little tourist shop. Beyond the shelves of tanning lotions and the racks of beach gear and swimsuits, he spotted the magazine stand. While Jenna headed for the refrigerated display of bottled water that they'd come in search of after a not-so-leisurely afternoon hike, Travis wandered over to the stand and felt his pulse quicken as he saw that *Chloe* magazine's October issue was on the shelves, complete with Jenna's article headlined on the cover.

Sure, he'd seen the complimentary copies of the magazine that Jenna had received, but there was something special about seeing it in a store, knowing her story was now out there in the world, being read by people everywhere.

He grabbed an issue from the rack and thumbed through until he found the right page— "Kill the Competition: Behind the Scenes in America's Not-So-Pretty Pageant Industry." No sooner had he read the title than the magazine was snatched from his hands.

"Hey, let me see that." Travis reached for the magazine, but Jenna evaded his grasp as she laughed and scanned the pages.

"Wait your turn."

"Better yet, you can share." He snaked his arm around her waist and pulled her against him as he read over her shoulder.

Her cocoa-butter scent reminded him of the adventures they'd had with tanning oil earlier that morning in their private garden. They were only in Maui for a quick stay before continuing on to Tahiti, but already he was considering extending the month-long trip by a week. Or two. Or six.

Images of Jenna frolicking on the beaches of the South Pacific wearing nothing but a sarong around her hips were making him think he was in for more fun than any one man should be allowed to have.

He spotted Jenna's byline, and his chest swelled with pride. Not even a gunshot wound had deterred her from her goal, and in the end, she'd written what he considered an article worthy of a Pulitzer. News of her ordeal had created a buzz about the article, and now Jenna had the luxury of picking and choosing the publications for whom she wanted to write.

"I still can't believe the story I stumbled into," Jenna said, shaking her head as she read.

"You didn't stumble—it just took you a while to figure out how big a story it really was."

The woman who'd shot Jenna had gotten away

with murder five years earlier and was convinced that Jenna was onto her. Andrea Patton, former Miss Golden State, had murdered the woman she'd considered her biggest competition by feeding her low-fat brownies laced with ground-up peanuts after she'd heard about the woman's severe peanut allergy. Andrea confessed to everything in an emotional breakdown at the police station, and Jenna had gotten a whole new angle for her story.

Not only had her career taken a turn for the better recently, but her relationship with Kathryn had blossomed, too. Travis couldn't help feeling partly responsible for the sisters' newfound friendship, and while he suspected they'd never be as close as many twins were, they seemed to have accepted their differences and learned to appreciate each other for the individuals they were.

Their families, on the other hand, were still coming to terms with everything. Kathryn and Jenna's parents had been rightly disturbed by the shooting. Jenna had resisted all her mother's efforts to baby her during her weeks of recovery, and she'd bristled at her mother's sudden shower of affection.

Travis's mother and father were still acting a little shell-shocked. First having their dreams of a perfect family wedding explode in a burst of gunfire, and then having not only Kathryn but also her twin sister, Jenna, join the family—Travis suspected it was a bit more than his mother could take without a good, stiff drink.

They'd been civil enough to Jenna, though, and she was much less concerned than Kathryn about his parents' approval. Travis didn't give a damn what the Roths thought, not now when he had found more happiness than he'd ever dared to imagine.

Jenna paid for the magazine and water, and they wandered hand in hand back out into the late-afternoon sunshine.

"Want to look into those windsurfing lessons now?" she asked when they passed an athletic shop with ads for lessons in the window. She'd been teasing him all week about his aversion to water sports.

"Tomorrow. We'll definitely do it tomorrow. After such a strenuous hike, I had something a little more intimate in mind for right now."

"Hmm. Intimate, you say?"

"You, me, the hot tub, a little sensual stress relief—for old times' sake?"

"It wouldn't be complete without a bottle of wine."

"I spotted a nice California red in the minibar this morning."

Jenna pulled him close and smiled a wicked smile. "Did I ever show you the *other* thing I know how to do with a good bottle of wine?"

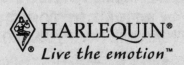

Silhouette Desire from *his* point of view.

BETWEEN DUTY AND DESIRE
by Leanne Banks
(Silhouette Desire #1599, on sale August 2004)

MEETING AT MIDNIGHT
by Eileen Wilks
(Silhouette Desire #1605, on sale September 2004)

LOST IN SENSATION
by Maureen Child
(Silhouette Desire #1611, on sale October 2004)

FOR SERVICES RENDERED
by Anne Marie Winston
(Silhouette Desire #1617, on sale November 2004)

Available at your favorite retail outlet.

If you enjoyed what you just read,
then we've got an offer you can't resist!

Take 2 bestselling love stories FREE!

Plus get a FREE surprise gift!

introduces an exciting new family saga with

DYNASTIES : THE DANFORTHS

A family of prominence... tested by scandal, sustained by passion!

Available at your favorite retail outlet.